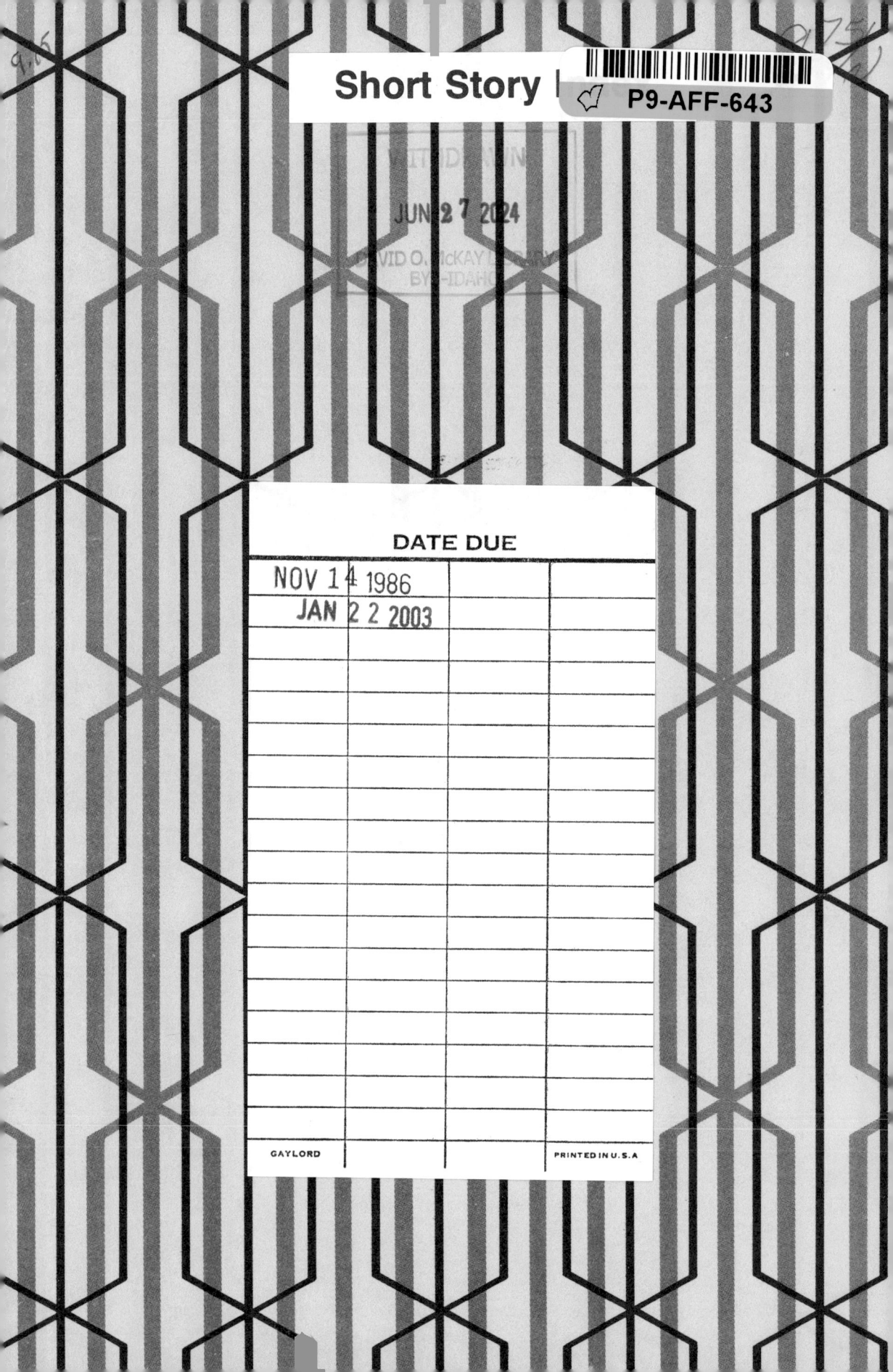

DATE DUE

NOV 14 1986		
JAN 2 2 2003		
GAYLORD		PRINTED IN U.S.A

BEHIND
MOROCCAN
WALLS

BEHIND
MOROCCAN
WALLS

TRANSLATED AND ADAPTED BY
CONSTANCE LILY MORRIS
FROM THE BOOKS OF
HENRIETTE CELARIÉ

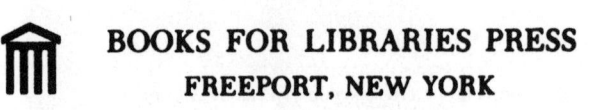

Short Story Index

WITH PICTURES BY
BORIS ARTZYBASHEFF

BOOKS FOR LIBRARIES PRESS
FREEPORT, NEW YORK

First Published 1931
Reprinted 1970

STANDARD BOOK NUMBER:
8369-3296-X

LIBRARY OF CONGRESS CATALOG CARD NUMBER:
74-106259

PRINTED IN THE UNITED STATES OF AMERICA

FOREWORD

This volume is made up of a selection of short stories from two volumes by Mme. Henriette Celarié, *Amours Marocaines* and *La Vie Mysterieuse des Harems*, Librairie Hachette, 1927.

They are sketches more than short stories, attempting to show without preamble cross-sections of native Moroccan women's lives, as told to and discovered by the alertly interested wife of a French officer living for years in that country.

Such as they are, each story, the author states, is rigorously true; only the names have been changed. Differing perhaps from the usual romantic picture, their flavor of reality can be even more impressive. This is Morocco, static, fluid, potential.

INTRODUCTION

During a recent journey to Morocco, I came across the stories of Mme. Henriette Celarié, which I felt so accurately depicted the life in Morocco, especially the secluded life of the women, that I asked permission of the authoress and the publishers of her books, Hachette and Co. of Paris, to translate and adapt some of these stories. I obtained this permission, and the accompanying stories are the result. They do not pretend to be a literal translation, as I was given permission to use the material very freely.

The stories were originally written by Mme. Celarié, the wife of a French officer in Morocco, who lived in that country for many years, often in obscure villages where the French have military stations. Under these circumstances, she had many opportunities to study the intimate life of the country at close range and the information with which her books are filled is very illuminating and accurate. I have selected stories from two of her books, entitled " Moroccan Love " and " The Mysterious Life of the Harems."

I wish to acknowledge with gratitude a debt I owe to Miss Elmira Grogan for assisting me in my work. Now at the time of publication of this book, I could not resist the desire to beg the Maréchal Lyautey, to be gracious enough to give me his patronage, on account of the brilliance which his name radiates in Morocco, as well as on account of the magnificent work of civilization which he accomplished there. I trust he will find expressed here the homage and sincere admiration of a friend of his country.

Paris, le 12 Novembre 1930

Madame,

        C'est bien volontiers que je viens vous assurer
de tout l'interêt que m'inspire votre ouvrage : BEHIND
MOROCCAN WALLS.

        L'adaptation que vous avez faite des livres de
Madame Henriette CELARIE rend bien la figure de ce Maroc
si grand par son caractère et ses traditions qu'il m'a été
donné d'attacher à la France, dans la mesure de mes moyens,
en des heures inoubliables.

        Certes, parmi les nombreux auteurs qui ont dépeint
les divers aspects de la vie Marocaine, Madame CELARIE est
de ceux qui se sont le plus distingués par une information
exacte et la compréhension d'un peuple si différent du nôtre
à certains égards.

        M'étant astreint moi-même à comprendre chaque jour
davantage la nature de ce peuple, vous n'aurez pas de peine
à discerner la sympathie profonde que m'inspire l'oeuvre
que vous avez entreprise et à laquelle je souhaite le plus

légitime des succès.

Daignez agréer, je vous prie, Madame, l'hommage de mes sentiments respectueusement dévoués.

CONTENTS

THE GIRL POSSESSED OF A DJINN

CHAPTER I

THE GIRL POSSESSED OF A DJINN

During the feasts attendant upon a native marriage I had chanced to make the acquaintance of Lella Mabrouka, wife of Si Ali ben Moktar. We passed the time together, talking and gossiping, and when she asked me, " Wilt thou honor me with an early visit? " I promised her I would.

The Ben Moktars are *chorfas*. Their family, once one of the wealthiest of the city, has long since fallen into decay. With a great leaning toward ostentation and no economy — it had not taken long to go through a fortune that had once been well established.

Si Ali ben Moktar, who is only thirty-eight years old and the possessor of perfect health, should certainly be able to work. There are numerous trades which an honest Marrakechi might take up — if only to conduct the winter tourists sight-seeing — but unfortunately a *cherif* cannot resort to work without feeling himself debased.

Then how do the Ben Moktars exist? — They live on charity.

Being *chorfas*, they receive a small income from the Habous. When that money is spent the wife and daughter of Si Ali know how to get more. Out in their patios they begin chanting the *surahs* of the Koran that recommend the giving of alms.

" Oh Believers! Pity consists not in turning thy face to the rising or the setting sun. Pious is he that believes in God and the last Judgment. . . . Who for the love of God shares his possessions with his kindred, with orphans, with the needy, with strangers and those who beg. . . . These are the just who will see the Father. . . ."

[3]

Their neighbors hear them and understand. One fetches a bit of tea, another some sugar, still another brings eggs and flour. The Ben Moktars have something to live on for a few days longer and render thanks to Allah. He alone is all-powerful.

The Ben Moktars' dwelling is beautiful and of lofty proportions. Scattered over the city there are several of these old houses unknown to tourists, that plunge those who are lucky enough to get inside them into raptures. But without funds to keep them up, everything in the house of the Ben Moktars is falling into ruin. Tiles are broken, stone floors worn, the paintings over the portals are faded by the sun and the carved cedar cornices are as bleached as bones. Sometimes, gazing at the desolation, Si Ali bolsters himself with the hope that some rich American will offer him a fabulous sum for it. " Then," sighs he, " if it be the will of Allah, we will be rich again. . . ."

The different rooms are in the same run-down condition as the patio. The niche of *el bahou* is bare of cushions, the rugs are worn down to the woof and the mattresses, whose wool is being sold bit by bit — as empty as *kessera*.

In his position of lord, Si Ali does as he pleases. He goes in and out, loiters in the *souks*, chats with a friend, looks on in the square of Djamaa el F'na at the many curious attractions — the fire-eaters, snake-charmers, tiny *chleuh* dancers with their suggestive gestures — or else seats himself on the mat of some Moorish café, shady in summer, warm in winter, and sips his glass of mint-flavored tea.

As for Lella Mabrouka, time passes for her in a far less diverting manner. Since the far-off day when she was veiled and which made her unutterably proud — for was she not lifted from the rank of little girl to womanhood? — she has left Marrakech only once, just one pilgrimage to a wise man in the *bled*.

This event took place shortly after her marriage. It made such a deep impression on her mind that she speaks of it as though it were yesterday. — " It was springtime. There were flowers of every color in the world. . . . I do love flowers. . . ."

I am unable to see why it is so constantly stated that Moslem women are contented with their lot. It depends entirely on the person. Those

[4]

like Lella Mabrouka find it a wearisome thing to be closed in forever by the four walls of an arid patio.

Oftentimes she says to me, " Render thanks unto Allah. Thy husband takes thee everywhere with him. Thou hast seen all the nations. There is a saying among us, ' He that has never soiled his *babouches* on the highway, should have *kohl* prepared for him.' (Be treated as a woman.) But Western women are the equal of men."

" Perhaps some day you, too, will go on a journey."

" *Ia*, if I only could! If I had the *flouss!* "

" Where would you choose to go, to Casablanca, to Fez? Or farther still, to France, to Paris? "

" I would journey to Mecca."

Lifting her eyes to heaven, she raises her hands with a naïve gesture — curved palms outward as though cupping a gift — adding, " Every day I pray to Allah to send *flouss* to Si Ali so that he can send me on a pilgrimage." Like most aging Moslem women, Lella Mabrouka is most pious.

By the six women he legitimately married and by the numerous slaves he possessed in the days of plenty, Si Ali has fathered twenty or twenty-two children. It would be useless to ask him to verify the number. He has forgotten it. He has them to suit all tastes, black, white, nigger. All of them died young except two, a son, Mohamed, and a daughter, Kheïra.

Kheïra is in the bloom of youth. It would be a difficult task to find a more enchanting face in all Marrakech. She has already learned to vivify her immense dark eyes with a little *kohl* purloined from her mother ; her skin is jasmin-white and she knows how to enhance its purity by the colored head veils she winds about her hair and whose tips she coquettishly leaves to dangle over one ear.

In any land it is hard for a poor girl, however beautiful she may be, to find an eligible husband. The difficulty is heightened in a Moslem country when the girl is born a *cherifa*. Custom demands that she marry a man of the same rank as herself. Certainly there is more than one at Marrakech, but the suitable ones, as is only natural, are seeking to add luster to their house by marrying a girl of wealth or of influential family. Kheïra had neither.

[5]

However, one " day of days," it seemed that fortune was beginning
to smile her way. By chance I happened to be visiting the Ben Moktars,
when an old woman entered the patio, a negress whom Kheïra rid of her
haik with exaggerated care. It was the *g'nafa*, Yakout.

The *g'nafas* play an important social rôle in Morocco. Mistresses of
ceremony when a family festival takes place, they have entrée to all the
homes ; going from one to another, they see and hear everything. Bearing tales, arranging matches between girls and young bachelors, they
carry on for personal profit, and sometimes for the happiness of the
young couples, a trade that rather closely resembles that of a go-between
with honorable intentions.

Yakout is installed in *el bahou* by my side. Her old back is propped
up with cushions and when the supper hour comes round, Kheïra places
on the little round table before her a savory mutton stew with carrots
and invites the old negress to dip her fingers in.

" Eat, little mother," Lella Mabrouka kept insisting. " If thou eat-
est nothing, I shall believe that thou dost not find it good."

When the old negress left she was not only well fed, but bore away in
her sleeve a generous *fabor* which her hostess had slipped to her in the
moment of farewells.

Nothing puts one in such a generous frame of mind as having a belly
and purse well lined. The very next morning Yakout betook her old
legs to the house of the Ben Messaouds, whose son was of age to " wear
the turban."

While sipping the tea which the mother of young Ali ben Messaou
had hospitably poured for her, and while nibbling at the fragile " gazelle-
horns " of finely ground almonds in a paste, the old crone, as though
unintentionally, turned the subject to Kheïra.

" Thou dost not know her? — A true child of Allah! The dove has
lent her its gentleness. Her voice is sweeter than sugar itself. . . ."

" Beautiful? " interrupts Lella Zohra.

" Oh fathers, what dost thou ask! — Her hair is black as an ostrich
plume, her eyes are borrowed from the gazelle and her slender neck from
the antelope."

While the negress was thus describing Kheïra's charms, her qualities

[6]

of good housewife — "She knows how to weave both wool and silk, to embroider like a fairy, to run a house," — Lella Zohra was listening with a seeming indifference that did not deceive a woman of such experience as the *g'nafa*. When she took her leave she never ceased, all through the city, to assess the value of the gifts which the Ben Messaouds would not fail to shower upon her if the affair were happily consummated.

I went to see Lella Mabrouka quite often. I was present again when, a few days later, the negress reappeared. She was expected with breathless impatience in the broken-down old house.

Lella Mabrouka went to meet her. "Greeting, Lella Yakout. Is all well with thee?"

"All is well, but I am weary. All day long my old bones must run from one house to another. The families I see! The homes I enter! They are so beautiful, so enormous, so rich. Oh fathers, that house of the Ben Messaouds! What a patio — the peacock has adorned it with his wing feathers. The rooms are like those of the Nazarenes, rugs and easy chairs — gilt ones from Oran! And the mistress of the house, Lella Zohra! What wisdom! Her tongue utters only wise words; she would cut off her wrist before she would do a wrong. There is one whose daughter-in-law will be happy. . . ."

"What age is her son?" interrupts Lella Mabrouka, palpitating with hope and curiosity.

"Si Ali? He was eighteen, I believe, 'at the last figs.' By the Prophet, thou canst not conceive of a more beautiful son of Adam than he. He has huge eyes, a tall figure and he is so well-dressed. *Ia*, what a house! It has everything in it that one could desire, and what a family! — I forgot to tell thee that Si Ali has two sisters — perfect lambs. The girl that gets him will have Allah to thank. . . ."

On and on the two old women gossiped. Each of them, mentally, pursued the visions that her imagination conjured up.

The sun sank from the sky. The *g'nafa* rose and unfolded her *haïk* to wrap herself in. A complicated business that, the heavy stuff must be draped over the shoulders, around the hips and folded in four thicknesses, just so, about the head.

[7]

"Oh my mother," cried Lella Mabrouka, "thou must not be going like this. Stay, thou must partake of the *couscus* with us."

Lella Yakout was only waiting for this invitation, but good breeding requires that one be begged. "The blessing of Allah upon thee, Lella Mabrouka, but I am ashamed to eat with thee so often."

"And I would be ashamed if thou shouldst refuse. . . ."

It so happened that the *couscus* was dry that evening; the broth had been measured sparingly and the lard even more so. A few snips of carrots and turnips sparsely decorated the white pyramid of *semola*. There was no *fabor*, either, at departure. The Ben Moktars were going through a difficult moment.

The *g'nafa* left them in high displeasure. It was easy to divine her thoughts. — The Ben Moktars were stingy. They were free with fine words because they cost nothing — but as for *flouss, machache!* (Nothing doing.)

What took place next day when she knocked at the Ben Massaouds' door, I later heard from Lella Zohra.

The old negress' pudgy face, instead of grinning as usual, was so forbidding that Lella Zohra was struck by it and gave the customary formula of greeting with some misgiving, "All is well with thee, Lella Yakout?"

"Oh misery! I am getting old — the great interior nerve has ceased to function. The least thing tires me. I have so many cares that they keep me awake at night. — Those Ben Moktars of whom I spake to thee — I've just seen their daughter again. And may Allah put a knot in my tongue, but she is not at all like I told thee. I had only seen her that first time by a little lamp that gave off less light than a match. Everything is so poor in their house! The very walls are falling into ruin. And even the women's *caftans* — what poverty! I wouldn't be seen in them myself. *Ia*, what did I say about Kheïra — Very well, but her eyes are nothing like as large as I thought. There is even one, oh my mother, that is a trifle crossed. Her nose is wide and it seems to me that she limps a little but she is so wily that she had hidden it from me at first. She is not at all the girl for Si Ali. 'Twould be a sin to give him such an ugly wife — he is so handsome himself."

[8]

"By the Prophet," approved Lella Zohra, "thou speakest truth."

. . . .

Kheïra fell into a great despair when this long-anticipated project fell through. It seemed to her that her one chance of marrying was gone. "Oh misery," she wept to herself, "I must die without knowing the caresses of a husband," and she pictured herself growing gray in the dilapidated dwelling, poorly fed by the neighbors' charity, deprived of the things that mean happiness to a woman, new *caftans*, henna, *kohl*, perfumes.

The weeks passed by. There was only left young Mohamed to bring a little gaiety into the lives of the Ben Moktars. With the freedom that the Moslems allow to all their sons as soon as they grow up, Mohamed had made a great friend of one of his near neighbors, young Kadour ben Ibrahim. Together they went to the Moorish and European cafés, and to the cinema. Kadour who had *flouss* paid his companion's way and when he came home the youth liked to dazzle his mother and sister with a recital of what he had done and all that he had seen.

Kheïra listened with dark looks ; her eyes had widened in their black circles and her round cheeks were sunken.

"Kheïra is not well," said her mother when I went to see them. "She eats nothing and sleeps badly. Someone must have given her the Evil Hand."

"Who could it be?"

"It is not difficult to guess. It's that Embarka ben Mohamed who lives opposite. Because she is so ugly she is jealous of my Kheïra."

"You must call in a doctor for the child."

"Why? If Kheïra is sick it is the will of Allah."

"But the doctor would cure her."

"She will be better when Allah wills it. Besides, I have made her wear amulets."

In spite of this precaution, Kheïra's state grew worse. Several times a day she was seized with sickness. Then her body grew rounder, her walk heavier, and it became evident that the girl's illness came from perfectly natural causes.

The Ben Moktars could no longer hide Kheïra's condition, but they grew heated against those who dared insinuate that their only daughter had found a lover. With that whimpering tone which the *caida* imposes on women for recounting their woes, Lella Mabrouka moaned,

"Oh my Lord Mohamed! Oh Merciful! — Be still — what dost thou dare to say? — My daughter! My own daughter whom I love ' as this eye and this eye ' — A *cherif's* daughter! Think a moment — In the first place no man enters here. The door is ever double-locked. Si Ali carries the key. . . . How could it have happened? — It is that Embarka." Her poor words tumbled over each other.

People avoided answering her, but in the other harems where I heard gossip about the Ben Moktars, the women mentioned, "Of course Kheïra does not go out — a *cherifa!* But there is the roof. The roof that gives access to the neighboring houses. In one of them dwells Si Kadour, the friend of young Mohamed. He knew Kheïra ; he has seen her and played with her before she was veiled. . . ."

Kheïra came into her eighth month. Because of her slender frame she appeared all the heavier. In vain she tried to hide her condition beneath the flowing *caftan.*

It was about this time that her parents found an explanation for the misfortune that had overtaken their daughter. Why had they not thought of it before? It had all come about through the malevolence of Embarka — that daughter of *Chitane* (Satan) — may her mother be accursed! She had thrown a spell on Kheïra. — A *djinn* had taken possession of the girl.

With nerves strained to the breaking point Lella Mabrouka shouted out this news exonerating her daughter, exonerating herself and all the tribe of Ben Moktar, issue of the Prophet. Her voice broke.

Blame Kheïra? What fault could it be of the child's? It would be better to think more about delivering her from the *djinn.*

This they proceded to do. One evening when I arrived at the house of the Ben Moktars I found the whole place in an uproar — tom-toms, *raitas*, castanets. Night tented darkly above the patio, but in the center of it a huge bonfire shed its reddish flickering glare. Squatting on the ground a group of *gnaouas* beat their immense drums and shook their heavy castanets.

[12]

One of them, the chief, seemed to be leading a Satanic festival. Old long since, his beard perfectly white, he spun around and around on one hardy leg, following the rim of the circle formed by his musicians, in the center of which stood Kheïra.

Drawn to her full height, her face darkly veiled by a thick silk, the girl stood immobile. Her arms hung loosely at her sides. A mauve and yellow scarf — her most beautiful scarf — bound her hair.

With great leaps, with an agility amazing in so old a body, the black approached her. He invoked Allah and Sidi Merzoug, patron saint of the *gnaouas*. His raucous voice filled the courtyard and dominated the bedlam of the castanets.

"May this *djinn* be cast out of this body which he has chosen to inhabit! — If these incantations fail, he must yield him to the power of perfume . . ."

The fire-lit shining ebon dancer drew a small phial from his flapping sleeve. He began to sprinkle the girl generously from it. The odor of jasmin mingled with that of the heavy incense that Lella Mabrouka was burning at the far end of the patio, next a heap of offal.

The *qarqbas* (castanets) beat more sharply. Making *gnaoua* magic without stint, the squatting musicians mingled their clamor with their chief's.

"Lord! Lord! In the name of the Lord! In the name of Sidi Merzoug!"

The old negro gave one mighty bound. The charm worked. I saw the girl move out of her daze. Still heavily veiled, she began to dance, or rather, to swing her body in a deep rhythm. Her arms lifted from her sides. The fire-glare deepened the hollows of her eyes and the pupils gleamed more ardently. She came toward me, straight toward me, a short, grotesque shadow, her own, dancing at her side.

For a second longer she kept moving very fast, her glance failing. Suddenly she fell as though from a blow back of the knees. . . .

Some weeks later, basking in the patio, Kheïra held on her lap a tiny baby swaddled like a mummy and covered with amulets against the Evil Eye which had proved so fatal to its mother.

[13]

With its sad black eyes, its dark skin and heavy lips, this *djinn's* son astonishingly resembled a certain Marrakechi well known to me and who is no other than young Kadour, friend of Si Mohamed ben Moktar, childhood friend of Kheïra and her neighbor.

"IN THE NAME OF ALLAH I DIVORCE THEE . . ."

CHAPTER II

"IN THE NAME OF ALLAH I DIVORCE THEE . . ."

There is bright sunlight flooding the square of *Djamaa el F'na*, a blinding sunlight, but Batoul's tiny house is dark and cold. Its walls are caked with dirty greenish flakes that look as though it had been attacked by some malady that commenced at the base and had corroded its way to the ceiling.

Batoul lives alone in her house. That is, without a husband, for the three other *koubbas* on the same patio, in the same building, are inhabited by neighbors. They are all lean people because *kessera* costs dear ; they are dirty because they only wash on Fridays.

Batoul has no love for them. " Do not go in there," she warns me. " They are queer, they have the Evil Eye. And their houses are full of fleas."

" Allah! Batoul, are you sure it is only fleas they have? "

My hostess' little leathery brown face lights up with a malicious smile. " Thou art right — they don't know what it means to clean up."

Batoul herself sweeps her *koubba* every morning. She has a little palm-leaf broom for this that bends her down nearly to the ground. Every morning, also, she shakes out her mattress and her cushions. Every morning? — Well, nearly every morning.

At whatever time of the day I arrive I am sure to find her home. " Streets are not made for a decent woman," she says loftily.

She spends her time weaving *burnouses*, *haiks*, or carpets. Wool is furnished her as she is too poor to buy it ; she gets paid only for her labor.

Batoul has placed the tea-urn, the painted tin containing the sugar, and all the tiny cups on a copper tray ; one might think we were children playing at dolls.

Batoul borrowed the copper tray and the cups, but the tea-urn is her own. A bunch of fresh mint as big as her two fists fills the small room with its scent of spring-time gardens. On a plate covered with pink gauze there are a few " gazelle-horn " pastries.

Batoul the economical, Batoul the poverty-stricken, does not often entertain. When she does she wants to give the impression that in her house you are in the household of a *tajer* (rich merchant).

While we wait for the water to boil, Batoul seats herself in front of me.

" Before this," she informs me, " I had a great big house. Thou couldst have eaten on the floor, it was so clean. I had jewelry of gold. They were so beautiful that they were rented for feast-days ; two *douros* for a pearl necklace ; a half *douro* for two bracelets. I bought *kohl* and perfumes with the money. I had silk and velvet *caftans*, I had *sebenias* and *ferragiats* — I had chests full of them."

Recounting these things, it is as if once again she held them in her hands ; her eyes glisten, she softly smiles.

I admonish her, " You must marry again, Batoul, and have a happy life ; then you would not be obliged to work all the time. You must marry again — you are young and healthy."

She draws herself up and throws me a black look.

" The blessing of Allah upon thee ! A husband to take the money I earn ! A husband to make me ' eat of the stick ' ? "

" Come now, Batoul, — just because you were not lucky with the first — "

" I don't know what thou meanest with thy ' lucky.' Allah had written it over me, that's all. . . . I was very small, my second teeth were not yet out, when my parents, my father, mother, uncles, aunts, ' went to the pardon of Allah.' They died the year of a great drought followed by a siege of typhus caused from the distress. At that time you could count that nine out of every ten inhabitants died."

" The blessing of Allah on thy head, Batoul. He will make thy reward greater in the Beyond — "

[18]

" May he change my affliction into resignation. He is the Master ! "

" Who looked after you, Batoul, who brought you up ? "

" A friend of my mother, a generous friend, Lella Fatma. She treated me as her own child, as a *cherifa*. She never would allow me to go out on the streets. If there came a knock on the door she did not even want me to go to answer it. When I reached marriageable age, she found a husband for me. I was then about twelve years old."

" At least it was a good marriage ? "

" It was a splendid marriage. Si Omar gave eight hundred *douros* as a *sadecq* and since I had little *flouss*, he said, ' I take on myself the expenses of the marriage and the trousseau.'

" All Lella Fatma's friends exclaimed, ' Glory to Allah for Batoul. — She was born with a palm-tree on her head (lucky).' "

Batoul was silent ; then with a little sneer,

" Si Omar knew what he was about. He had been told that I was clever at embroidering and cooking. He thought to himself, ' The *sadecq* cost me dear but at least I will have a woman capable of running my house.' "

The marriage feasts were held. The moment arrived when henna is put on the *arousa* (the bride) and the women surround her, singing the sacred chant,

> " May Mohamed give a *koubba* unto the *arousa*
> To reign therein . . ."

Soon after, the mule sent by the bridegroom arrived at the door. One last time Batoul crossed the patio, the passageway of the house that had been her shelter. The little girls shouted, " you-you," and the boys sang,

> " By my father, I would desire thee myself,
> But thou art not for me ! "

When she was enveloped in the " veil of pride " (bride's veil), she was mounted on her mule. It was nearly midnight. The women formed her escort across the city. The air sounded with their shouts of joy. Those were her last happy moments.

Batoul entered a new life. Her husband, Si Omar, still had his mother.

"Thou knowest her?" Batoul demanded of me.

"I have never seen her."

"Allah has been good to thee! Never try to meet her. Lella Malika? — She is more wicked than a daughter of *Chitane* (Satan). I had to live with her. At first this seemed all right. I was young; I needed counsel. But my mother-in-law greeted me — I beg your pardon but it is thus we say it — as one greets the stomach-ache."

"She was jealous?"

"Oh my father, the Nazarenes know everything! — Thou hast seen the cause at once. Living with a mother-in-law whom you detest is worse than hell."

"I don't doubt it."

"No, thou canst have no idea of it! What I have had to bear from her passes human imagination. Ye *Roumiyas*, ye are free; ye do not know what it is to be closed in from morning to evening in the same walls with someone who spies on every word, every movement, and then gives a twisted account of it.

"When I asked Si Omar to let me go to the *hamman*, the baths, he answered, 'Go.'

"My mother-in-law accompanied me. When we returned she ran to her son.

"'Si Omar, listen — In the streets Batoul half opened her *haik;* she let a man see her face. He was young and well-dressed. . . .'

"If I went up on the roof in the evening to breathe a bit as we all do, Lella Malika mounted at my heels. Scarce were we down again than she was hissing in what teeth were left to her, words of hate to Si Omar. 'A man passed in the street — I saw him. He looked upon Batoul and raised his eyes to heaven. — She answered him by slightly raising the hem of her *caftan*.'

"Things continued this way for a long time. Oh my father, she left me nothing. — It was as if she had dragged me over the carding-board."

"You could have proved your innocence."

" What sayest thou! — Men are by nature so suspicious that they accept all accusations. And then, among our people, mothers have power over the characters of their sons. They are always like children in their hands. They obey them in everything. Thou knowest our saying, ' If thy father calls thee whilst thou art at prayer, continue as if nothing had happened ; but if it be thy mother, hasten for women are irritable and it is not well to waken the anger of thy mother.' "

On the small *kanoun*, the water boils in the tea-kettle. Batoul springs up, pours it in the urn where she has tightly stuffed the tea and mint. She tastes the decoction, pours it back in the pot, sugars it, tastes it again, gives me a glass. Then while I drink it in the proper little sips, she resumes,

" Listen still to this : I was with child. This pregnancy should have bound Si Omar closer to me. Oh my misfortune! It served but to sever us. Lella Malika continually repeated to her son, ' Batoul has a lover. The child she expects is not thine. Everybody knows it.' "

Just accuse a woman unjustly. — You will hear her respond if she has any blood in her veins and praise to her for it. Batoul is like that. She is savage besides and hot-hearted. She defended herself. Her husband beat her.

I asked, " Why did you stay there, Batoul? Why did your husband keep you? If he had no confidence in you he could have divorced you."

" Wait, thou wilt understand. One day among days, and when I was near my time, Si Omar made a scene more violent than those that had preceded it. He cried at me,

" ' Thou hast a lover, I know it. Dog, may thy bones rot!'

" His eyes rolled in his head with rage. I shrieked,

" ' Madman, thou liest in thy teeth!'

" He shouted all the louder. The insults that I heard! It was like a hail of stone thrown over me."

At the end Batoul lost her head. When her husband repeated to her for the hundredth time, " Thou hast a lover — I am sure of it!" — she cried back in exasperation,

" Since you hold to it so strongly, well, yes then, I have a lover and my child is his!"

[23]

She had scarcely got the last word out when the door of the room was pushed open. Two strange men entered. Batoul had just time to turn herself to the wall to prevent them from seeing her face. These men were *adouls* or lawyers. Si Omar himself had posted them in the patio ; he had provoked the quarrel with his wife only to bring about the thing that had occurred.

" A trap that he set for me," she explains, " a trap into which I fell."

The *adouls* spoke to Batoul. " We have put in writing the statement we have just heard from your own lips."

" My heart was beating in my breast," sighs Batoul, " like a wounded dove. I cried out,

" ' Ye have not done such a thing — What I said is a lie. I was beside myself. How could I have a lover ! How could I have sinned thus? Ye must believe me — I have never lied. I could not if I tried.'

" They sneered, ' May the sea be over thee ! At this very instant thou hast lied. To Si Omar thou sayest, " I have a lover." To us thou swearest, " I have none." ' They held themselves upright in front of the door like two pillars of a mosque. And I continued my defense,

" ' If ye are wise men, ye ought to read in my heart, my spirit. Ye have heard me ; my voice was not that of a woman in her senses — '

" But the *adouls* were in my husband's pay. They replied with terrific sternness,

" ' We have written down your own statement.' "

Though Batoul pleaded with them, her protests were " as a wind in a cage " ; there was nothing left for her to do but gather her belongings together and depart within the hour. Lella Fatma, the friend who had brought her up, again offered her shelter.

I say, " This was surely the end of your misfortune? "

" The end of my misfortune ! Allah had not decreed it so. Each day the midwives sent by Si Omar came to visit me. When my time came, they installed themselves beside me and as soon as the child was born they took it and bore it to my husband."

" To your husband? But he pretended the child was not his ! "

" He had said that in order to divorce me without paying alimony. How could he have denied the child? The little thing resembled him as much as if he 'had blown it through his nose.' Besides, what could I have done? The child was a boy ; the child 'belongs to the couch.' And then Si Omar was wily. He put before the *cadi* the fact that the baby would be ill cared for because I had no means of support. The *cadi* granted him his rights. Allah is master! — He alone knows what became of the *moutatchou !* "

"Batoul," I cried, "you do not mean to say that you have never seen your child?"

She was pouring fresh tea into my glass ; she did not interrupt her task, she did not look up at me, and in the most natural tone she let fall a word that pierced my heart,

"Never."

A CHILD'S KIDNAPPING

CHAPTER III

A CHILD'S KIDNAPPING

Not far from the house of my friend Batoul, and at the end of a long blind alley in the Kessaria, appears the passage that leads to the dwelling of Lella Massaouda ; its steep ascent forms a series of long, high steps. If one can manage to mount them they give at last onto her patio. A shimmering marvel of a patio, this one, displaying on walls and floor, square, antique tiles whose countless rosettes gleam in tones of gold and turquoise.

Lella Massaouda has insisted that I take my seat in *el bahou*. *El bahou* is the recess in the wall found in almost all native homes. A very cultivated gentleman of my acquaintance has told me that our alcoves are copied from them. "In the time of the Crusades," he says, "our ancestors — " But I will spare you his development. . . .

In *el bahou* the guest of honor finds mattresses and cushions arranged for his comfort and from his nook in the midst of them enjoys a complete view of the patio and its fountain of singing water.

The sunless day is about to die. It is cold, very cold. In a tiny porcelain *kanoun* a few embers, reddening fitfully, give off a feeble heat. An old negress, the *dada*, is the only one permitted to profit by its warmth. My hostess belongs to the *Maghzen* world and follows its traditions. "Fire," she says, "is to look at, not to approach."

Short of leg, with a great stomach falling down over her thighs, the *dada* looks like a slave who has long since forgotten privations. The stuff of which she is made is not the beautiful thin material, fine and white, which served for her mistress ; it is a black stuff, rather coarse, but solid, resistant. It has served for a long time already ; for a long time hereafter it will be in use.

[29]

The *dada* nursed Lella Massaouda's eldest son. She is a slave but treated as a friend of the family. She herself has no feeling of being an inferior. When I arrived she offered me her hand with the rest of them. At the present moment, seated beside her mistress, she prepares the tea, offers me the cakes and nods approval when Lella Massaouda enjoins me,

"Eat for thy good and thy health."

Back near the silver samovar, squatting easily on her heels, she looks at me — she knows that it is because of her I have come. I wait. She seems to be arranging her thoughts inside her big wooly head. Then,

"So, thou wouldst have me weep again, since thou demandest that I tell thee my history?"

A tiny girl playing in the patio has heard what the *dada* just said; she slips to the open door; under her *ferragiat* she wears a *caftan* green as grass which falls clear to her feet; her black hair is parted and hangs in two long tresses on either shoulder. She peeps into the room; she dares not enter without a word of permission. She turns to her grandmother, Lella Messaouda, calling softly,

"Apple of my eye, apple of my eye — precious — "

Lella Messaouda answers, "Come in, my little tiny one, my little moon."

The child approaches us; she squats down on the mattress back of the *dada*. Nestling there with her tiny smile, she looks, being so round and so soft, like a big and very contented cat. She looks as if she might go "purr-purr" if she were stroked.

The voice of the old *dada* breaks in the stillness. I write it down just as she speaks. I write it exactly, without altering a word. It is she you hear, in her slightly husky voice. . . .

"First of all I must say that in the *douar* where my parents lived and which is in the *Sous*, no kidnapping of little girls had ever taken place. My parents were not *meskines*. They owned several cows and cultivated their fields. At home I helped my mother about the housekeeping, I ground the grain in the hand-mill, I fetched water from the *oued*, I gathered wood in the forests for the fire.

"My father had a single sister who was thus my aunt. She lived

[30]

at *Stouka*. Her husband had but lately betaken himself to the pardon of Allah. My aunt would have wished to come to see us but she was afraid to leave her house; she had five daughters and in the region of *Stouka* little girls were often stolen to sell as slaves.

"So my father said, 'It is up to us to bear her our condolences.'

"I started out in company with my father, my mother, and my two brothers. The eldest, Mohamed, was older than I, the other, M'hamed, was younger. My mother was with child; I recall that she was in her ninth month, and I might add that I had had a sister who had been killed during an uprising which had taken place in the country some little while before. A stray bullet had struck her.

"In the region where my aunt dwelt there are only drifts of sand high as small mountains and wild Barbery figs. After a long trip — we had traveled for six days and always afoot — we reached her house.

"That evening of my arrival, I went with my aunt's daughters to gather wood for the fire. I was the smallest of the band. We were scattered in the thickets. It was still day but night was falling. I remember that all the while we searched for twigs and branches, we were singing. You ask what song? —

"'Oh my father, oh my mother, guard me well.
If a bandit came to steal me, he would bear me away to Moghreb —
Thou wouldst weep and I would weep. . . .
Oh my parents, remember that my tears
Would flood the valleys and the plains. . . .'"

The *dada's* voice, so rough a moment since, yields itself to moving modulations.

Behind her comes a sound of sobs. It is little Mina, moved to pity. In the patio, sonorous and empty, the fountain, straight as a sword of silver, weeps with her. It seemed to be rivaling Mina to see which of the two could be saddest.

Lella Massaouda turns around. She draws her grandchild to her, takes her on her lap.

"Weep not, my little moon. . . ."

[31]

"'Apple of my eye,' it is the tale the *dada* tells — "

"Go play."

"'Apple of my eye,' let me stay. . . ."

The old *dada* is arranging the cups on the copper tray.

"Go on, *dada*."

Mina has dried her eyes. Protected by her grandmother, she is now full of courage to bear the sufferings of another. She listens with all ears, with little, gaping mouth.

"Behind the wild fig trees," resumes the *dada*, "there were three men. They caught hold of me, they fastened their big hands over my mouth ; my cousins must not even have noticed my abduction. I alone was carried off.

"I do not remember how long we took to get to Agadir. One of the men wore a white *burnous*. With a corner of this *burnous* he protected me from the cold during the night. He was the cause of my misfortune, but because he showed pity on me, I nestled against him as if he had been my father.

"They gave me *kessera* and *zamita* to eat. Thou askest what *zamita* is? It is toasted flour sprinkled with sugar. It is very good. All that day we traveled ; at night we slept under the sky ; sometimes a star flashed across the heavens — I was afraid because shooting stars are darts thrown by the keepers of Paradise against the wicked spirits that prowl by night.

"From Agadir we journeyed to Souira, always afoot. When you come toward Souira you see the town, quite small, quite white and surrounded by the sea on all sides except one. The men took me to one of the notables in the hope of selling me. We went to his office. He was customs administrator.

"He was a Fasci. He said, 'If I bought her it would not be for myself ; I would send her to my family in Fez.'

"He had a great fat belly. How old was he? His beard was white. He looked me over, my teeth, my joints ; he felt my breasts and judged the firmness of my body. I wept the whole time, 'Bouh! Bouh!' The Fasci finally bought me. I cried so hard that he kept saying, 'She will go crazy!'

[32]

"I tell thee of a truth, Oh little mother, thou wouldst have believed that my blood was going to flow out of my eyes. I ceased to eat. I thought only of my parents.

"Then they made me get on board ship. On this ship was a young man whom they had also stolen to sell. He was so outraged that he could not even speak.

"We were on deck. There was only sky and water to see. It was the first time I had been to sea, but I was not afraid. One place was the same then as another to me.

"We reached Safi. Thou wouldst know if it was beautiful? — I was young, I had so much sorrow, I do not remember.

"They carried me to Fez and I arrived at my master's house. They were *tajers*. In their house were fine tiles and carpets. Ten years I remained with them. The husband had but one single wife; she seemed to me a trifle mad. Her lip hung down and when she spoke she reminded me of a bleating sheep. But she fed me well; she never struck me. Being a rich household there were other slaves and all of them were good to me.

"What had I to do, thou askest? I ran errands, I stayed near my mistress; when I grew up I learned to cook.

"But my mistress was so stupid I could not love her, and then there was another slave in the kitchen. — Since she was older than I she wished to rule me. I could not stand that. I asked my master to sell me. I was taken to the house of a slave-dealer. These dealers always have negresses in their houses destined to be sold.

"A certain Fasci had given the dealer an order to notify him when he had a young slave knowing this and that. The dealer thought I would suit. He led me to Si Mohamed's house. Evening had come. The candles in the room were lit in their silver candlestands. The house was large and beautiful.

"Si Mohamed said to me, ' Dost thou know how to cook, dost thou know how to sweep a room, canst thou sew?'

"I responded, ' I swear on my head I do not know.'

"Why did I answer ' I do not know '? — Because I could not pretend to know how to do everything perfectly and because I was afraid the other slaves in the house might do these things better than I.

[35]

" Then my master ordered two pullets to be brought. To me he said,
" ' Now cook them.'

" I cooked them. He ate of it and found it good. In the following
days he had me cook other sorts of *tagines*. I cooked them well and
for a week, every day, he ordered something new of me. When he found
that I was energetic and hard working, he bought me.

" Later on he came to live here at Marrakech. ' One day of days '
I met up with my cousins in the *souks*. They knew me again. They
said, ' Wilt thou not come home with us? '

" What would I have done there? My father, my mother, had both
gone to the pardon of Allah. My brothers — I did not know them.
Allah had placed me in this home. I answered my cousins,

" My masters have become my true parents. Leave me — I shall
die among them. . . ."

Little Mina slept on her grandmother's knee. The *dada's* history
no longer interests her. But the fountain continues to weep. Cut
precisely through the middle like a cheese, the half-moon lightens the
patio. . . .

BATOUL EXPLAINS HOW A WOMAN DECEIVES HER HUSBAND

CHAPTER IV

BATOUL EXPLAINS HOW A WOMAN DECEIVES HER HUSBAND

There is a question I burn to ask, but which I would never dare put to one of the old *Lellas* who pass the greater part of their time, running a chaplet through their fingers, mumbling, " Indulgence, Indulgence," or " Blessing, Blessing. . . ."

They would be shocked and would exclaim with horror-stricken faces, " Oh my master, what are you talking about? Such things do not happen — "

But Batoul lives near by, Batoul who has not reached the age where one weighs each word and pretends to be scandalized. It is not necessary to go around the point with her.

" Listen, Batoul. How can a woman among you deceive her husband? It cannot be easy. The houses are so shut-in, the women so well guarded — "

Batoul listens to me with a malicious grin. She is squatting on her heels before a primitive sort of loom which she has concocted herself with the help of a few reeds. For protection from the Evil Eye she has hung from it a " Hand of Fatma," a horse-shoe, several little leather bags of herbs, and a sheet of paper bearing verses of the Koran written out by a *fqih*.

Her nimble fingers come and go above the warp as over the cords of a harp. Swiftly moving, they lift the threads and deftly knot the ends of strings. Like all weavers, Batoul works on the wrong side and it is I who see the pattern emerge with its green and orange lozenges on a purple ground.

"Oh my turtle-dove," sighs Batoul, "women have ruses. They have plenty of them. The simplest are the best. Here is one. . . .

"The wife says to her husband, 'I should like to go to the baths.'

"Now to go to the baths is one of the things a husband dares not refuse. So he says, 'Thou desirest to go to the baths? — Go, then.'

"Needless to say, among *tajers* the woman possesses at least one slave. What would the *Lella* do without this slave — I ask thee! It is she who carries messages, buys the ointments, and the perfumes that the *Lella* desires without the knowledge of her husband, she who arranges the rendezvous. This slave almost always is old; she has brought up the young woman, she loves her, she has been part of her dowry and the husband has confidence in her.

"That confidence is well placed. — What would you expect? — The slave goes out to find her mistress' lover.

"'At such a time, in such a place, we will meet thee.'

"The *Lella* has made herself ready. She has put on her *haik*, she leaves the house; her old slave follows her, carrying the necessaries for the bath, for the young woman is careful to go to the *hammañ*, on account of the possible surveillance of her husband.

"But, instead of loitering at the baths as usual, to enjoy the pleasure of gossiping with her friends, she says, on the contrary, 'My time is short to-day.'

"Rapidly some *kobs* of hot water are dashed over her, she is massaged, and then she sets forth to meet her lover."

This honest little Batoul — after all, she is a woman! In speaking of other people's good fortune, her eye brightens, her lips move, on her young face appears the reflection of another desire.

"She meets her lover, you say? Where? At his house?"

"At his house? Allah — that would be too great a risk! — However, even that happens. Listen: no later than yesterday I met in the *souks* a daughter of one of my friends. She was all excited. She said to me, 'For a year my brother has been bringing one of his friends to the house. My mother and I always retired to our quarters, but yesterday my father returned unexpectedly. He went into my brother's room for some reason. The so-called friend was a woman ; she wore a *djellaba*, woolen socks, yellow *babouches*, and we guessed nothing ! ' "

This digression ended, Batoul returned to her first story.

" The *Lella* arrives at the rendezvous ; her lover is waiting for her. He has nicely arranged the samovar and the tea-urn and — as most frequently happens, — he has bought bottles of liquor. They drink together, they spend an agreeable time — "

I thought to myself : if it were her husband instead of her lover, he would bore her ; if she were his wife instead of his mistress, he would not find her beautiful and perhaps could not endure her. It is the same in all countries under heaven, where Allah has created man and woman seeking a change.

But Batoul continues,

" However, evening comes on and she must return ; she is intoxicated and she smells of alcohol and her husband is certainly home from the *souks*. Happily the *Lella* has her old slave's cunning to help her.

" On the very doorstep the *Lella* begins to groan. ' Oh my father, how my head hurts ! The water was too hot at the baths. Look, my forehead is all wet.' (She doesn't add that she had just been running, the wily creature !)

" Her husband is sorry for her. ' Here, take one of the pills that the *toubeba* gave you.'

" ' Why should I take a pill ? If I am sick it is the will of Allah. I shall recover when Allah pleases.'

" She lies down on a mattress. The slave covers her with a woolen rug so that the odor of alcohol will not pervade the room ; she lights a fire of sandal-wood whose fumes will mask that of the spirits.

" The woman goes off to sleep. Her intoxication wears off. In the morning she is fresh and rested. She says to her husband,

" ' It has done me good to sleep. That bath was really too hot.'

" What does the husband answer ? What wouldst thou have him answer ? — He believes his wife of course. He is as if she had put a spell over his eyes. He simply says,

" ' *Ourrah*.' "

In order to hunt a certain shade among the wools, at her right, Batoul interrupts herself. She is bending down, turned a little away. I can see only her profile ; a ray of light gilds her cheek and lends it a shimmer of nut wood freshly polished ; her features are a trifle sharp but pleasing.

I think over what she has just told me. Undoubtedly lack of liberty develops a spirit of cunning in human beings. This axiom is not a new one, but Batoul would never admit it. To listen to her, a husband was made to be deceived.

" Here is a story," she begins. " I don't know whether it is true. It is a very old one.

" A certain woman had an excessively jealous husband. Not once did he go out without locking her in and carrying away the key of the house. On his return he would ask a hundred suspicious questions.

" ' Did anybody knock at the door? Who was it? Was it really a beggar? Didst thou answer, " Allah will open to thee " ? — 'Naught else? — Swear it by the Prophet ! '

" The result was that his wife, who had never thought of deceiving him, began to search for means of doing so. It was not easy. ' One evening among evenings ' she went up on her roof. It was spring-time. The sinking sun spread on the sky such a bedizening as for a marriage *caftan*. Its colors were blinding. The woman half closed her eyes ; this did not prevent her from catching sight of one of her neighbors.

" He, too, saw her. They exchanged signals. The husband was gone. The woman whispered across, ' Listen. Every day from now on, water the ground in front of thy front door.'

" ' Why water it? '

" ' Thou wilt understand later. If thou doest exactly as I say I will reward thee.'

" Several days passed. The woman went to her husband.

" ' I want to go to the Moorish baths.'

" ' Very well, you may go.'

" He takes all the customary precautions. Orders the slaves designated to carry the *kobs*, the towels, the soap, to prepare themselves ; commands the eldest of them and the one in whom he has most confidence to watch over the *Lella*, not to let her out of her eye. He hires the entire Moorish bath so that his wife may meet no friend there who might give her bad counsel. A little before midnight the expedition sets out. One of the slaves goes before with a lantern. The women are burdened with all the bathing utensils; the old slave is at the *Lella's* side. The latter takes a few steps. Now she is before the house of her neighbor. The ground is well watered as she had recommended. She slips and falls. Her *haïk* is spattered with mud; she pretends to have hurt herself. She begins groaning,

"'Oh misery! I have broken my foot!'

"Her husband, who hears the outcry, rushes to help her. When he tries to touch her she groans all the louder. The neighbor's door opens. The neighbor is careful not to show himself but his women slaves rush to the *Lella* and beseech her to enter. She whispers weakly,

"'The blessing of Allah upon all of ye,' and with many cries she allows herself to be carried over the threshold by the women. The door closes after her.

"Some hours later she returns home. Her husband is waiting for her. She no longer has the air of a sufferer. The husband asks,

"'Nothing wrong?'

"'Nothing.' She smiles.

"'Why dost thou smile?' demands the husband.

"She acts as though she did not hear him and asks,

"'Thou still hast the key of the house?'

"He replies, 'Yes.'

"She laughs the more. 'Fool! Fool!'

"She dares not add, 'That's what thou art now! — That's what thou art!'

"The husband is so stupid he would not understand anyway. . . ."

Batoul herself laughs shamelessly. Quickly she regains her gravity. There is a moral and she was about to forget it:

"Against a woman's guile there is naught to be done!"

.   .   .   .

With the help of a heavy lead comb, Batoul compresses the woof she has just knotted on the warp of her rug; with large scissors she shears the wool.

"Batoul, do you know any other stories?"

[43]

Sententiously, she does not respond directly.

"Stories are like toasted almonds," she lets fall. "Some like them and ask for more. Some don't care for them at all."

"Batoul, I adore toasted almonds."

"Allah love thee! — I have a *chouari* full of them!

.   .   .   .   .   .

"A certain man was married. He had only one wife and *Chitane* (Satan) — may his name be accursed — tempted her to sin. Each night she took advantage of her husband's slumber to go to her lover.

"One time among many, the husband woke up. His wife was not at his side! He gets up, goes out, walks to the passageway. The street door has been left unbarred.

"'Allah! Allah!' he cries — 'That dog of a woman is outside!'

"He bars the door inside and waits. Toward the end of the night the woman attempts to get in. She pushes on the door — it resists.

"'Oh misery,' she thinks, 'I am caught.'

"At the same moment her husband's voice comes from the window above.

"'Carrion! Loose woman! Prostitute —'

"She does not answer his insults. She humbles herself and begs,

"'Open to me, my lord! Open to me!'

"'Open to thee! — I want all our neighbors to see thee at the door. They will know then how thou hast passed the night; they will know what a shameless creature thou art. . . . Dog!'

"The minutes speed by. The sky lightens. Soon it will be the hour of the first prayer. In each minaret the voice of the *muezzin* will proclaim mournfully the burial of another night, then salute joyfully the birth of another day. Believers will be going to their prayers. The woman thinks to herself,

"'I would rather die than be seen outside my own door. I absolutely must win my way in.'

"She studies how to do it. There is a well in the street outside. There is no well-curb — it is an Arab well. Not far from it stands a large boulder — the woman catches sight of it.

'As Allah wills it, I am saved!'

[44]

" She knows now what to do.   She pretends the most violent despair.

" ' My lord, open to me! I beseech thee! If thou dost not open I am going to throw myself into the well! '

" Behind the portals the husband sneers, ' That will be one dog less in the world! ' . . .

" ' Oh my master, thou hast forced me to it! . . .'

" She raises the stone and throws it in the well.

" The husband hears the splash of water — ploc!, ploc! . . .

" Softly he opens the door ; he pushes his head through, throws a glance down the street.   He fails to see his wife who is hidden behind a wall.

" ' Allah! ' he whispers, ' Allah! '

" He creeps to the well and leans over it.

" This is what his wife was waiting for.   She dashes to the house, bars the door, and when her husband tries to get in, it is she who refuses to open.

" ' Drunkard,' she shouts, ' companion of harlots! Is it thus thou livest?   See, oh ye people of good faith coming to prayer, how my husband behaves. . . .'

" In vain he protests.   No one believes him ; for many months it is he who must bear the public shame."

.　　.　　.　　.　　.　　.

These old stories, recalling those gusty ones of our ancestors in the Middle Ages, seldom fail to bring a laugh in native homes.   But at this point Batoul touches on a more delicate chapter, that of unmarried girls.

" ' In our circles,' the high-caste Moroccans say, ' young girls are held to the greatest modesty, the deepest reserve.'   The *caida* rules that they should see no women other than those who belong to their own family.   Should a friend of their mother, even, come as a guest, the young girl rarely puts in an appearance.

" So many precautions have but one end — to safeguard their purity. In Arabian countries the chastity of the *arousa* is one of the essential conditions to the contract of marriage.   The phrase in which the father of the groom couches his formal demand specifies this :

" ' I ask of thee thy daughter with her virginity, according to the traditions of Allah and the Prophet.'

[45]

" To which the father responds, ' I give to thee my daughter with her virginity, according to the tradition of Allah and the Prophet.'

" There are many, however, who on the day of marriage will have to resort to strategy to persuade their husbands that they still possess what they no longer have.

.   .   .   .

" Oh my fathers," exclaims Batoul, " women are so wily that the very wisest can be fooled by them ! "

I ask, " Batoul, what does the husband do when the *arousa* — "

" That depends on his class. If he is a man of high caste and loves his wife, he keeps her for fear of scandal ; otherwise he forces her to remount the mule that brought her and return to her parents. For him, he seeks the *cadi* who breaks the contract and fixes the amount of indemnity due a man in such a situation.

" A young girl," Batoul goes on, " never goes out alone. A slave or a relative of respectable age always accompanies her."

I had noticed this and ask how, then, since she never sees a man, is she able to fall in love with one.

" How? She has seen him from her roof ; she has met him in the street, smiled at him — he responded. He returns again to the spot where he met her, she goes back up to her roof, he is watching for her. Taking advantage of the isolation, they exchange a few words. Have you never noticed anything like that going on? "

" Heavens, no."

" It was because thou wert not warned of it. Pay attention — there will come more than one time when the street is deserted that thou wilt see a young man who appears to thee to be drunk, crazy even. He will seem to be talking to himself in a very loud voice. — High up on some roof, concealed by the parapet, a girl is listening to his words."

" What does he say to her? That she is beautiful — "

" The fact that he has picked her out, proves that. Later on he will repeat to her how he loves her, he will caress her with tender names — ' My perfumed couch, my golden butter — my honey in the honey-comb — '

" More often the lovers content themselves with exchanging signs ;

[46]

BORIS
ARTZYBASHEFF

to lift the eyes to heaven with a gesture of the hand that seems to embrace the whole horizon, means, ' Thou art everything to me!'

" To answer by lifting the hem of the *caftan* or waving a kerchief signifies, ' I accept thy love.'

" To converse by signs from afar is a charming game, but the lover soon gets enough of it. Sentimentality is not his strong point. He is an Arab, a Moroccan Arab, terribly realistic.

" Through his mother, his sisters, his slaves, he tries to get information. Discreetly he asks what old women have access to the house of his beloved. He hears their names. He gets the names, too, of several of the wily, grasping Jewesses who slip into houses with their baskets of kerchiefs and perfumes.

" The young man seeks out one of these *kaouadas*. ' I would have thee bear a message to Lella Fatma or Lella Zeïneb — ' he says.

" The old woman puts on a reproving mien. ' Don't count on me. If her father or her mother found me out I would be beaten and haled before the judge.'

" ' Thou hast nothing to fear. I know Lella Fatma. Simply say that you come from me, Si-Mohamed.'

" Still the old woman resists. ' Ah *sidi*, thou knowest the teeth of the powerful are pointed and the weak are eaten — '

" But the youth slips her a *fabor*. Then the *kaouada* feels an infinite kindness flood her heart. Why did she say just now that she might not be able to speak with Lella Fatma? Nothing would be easier. Besides, this tale of love which promises to be enriching interests her. It recalls the time of her youth when she herself was a ' daughter of joy.'

" When the young lover continues, ' Thou wilt ask Lella Fatma at what hour I may meet her,' the *kaouada* replies,

" ' The blessing of Allah and happiness be upon thee, oh *sidi;* luck is thy playmate. Thou shalt see her whom thou desirest!'

" She betakes herself to the beloved's dwelling. She is taken into the patio, into one of the rooms. She displays her wares. The slaves swarm about her and with cries of delight, jostling each other, admire the many lovely things which can never be for them. The mistress of the house fingers the silks and muslins.

[49]

" This is her chance. The *kaouada* approaches the young girl and slips into her ear, ' I am charged with a message for thee. Si-Mohamed has made me swear to speak of it to none but to thyself. Swear in thy turn that thou wilt repeat nothing, even to thy mother, of what I am going to tell thee.'

" ' Fear nothing. My mouth will be sealed so tightly not even a fly could enter.'

" ' Listen, then. — Si-Mohamed wishes to take a cup of tea with thee.'

" The girl understands this message. She lowers her lids quickly so that none may see the sparkle of her eyes. She responds,

" ' Thou wilt say to Si-Mohamed that I give him *salaam* ; but he must know that it is impossible for me to take tea with him. I am not allowed to go out.'

" The go-between returns to the young man. He rushes to her.

" ' What news? '

" ' The turtle-dove may not go out alone.'

" Si-Mohamed raises his shoulders. ' Allah! Allah! She is playing with me and thee both! That pretext is not serious. Tell her that if she loves me she will arrange a way to meet me.'

" The wily old crone listens solemnly. She sees now with what ardor Si-Mohamed desires Lella Fatma ; but it would not do for them to meet too quickly ; she must get further *fabors* out of this.

" Joy dancing in her heart, she affects an air of great concern and replies sedately, ' Grant me a little more time ; that which thou wishest is not easy and I must think over a means to employ.' "

. . . . . .

Thus far Batoul had come with her tale when the outer portal of the house opened and then closed. I heard on the flagstones of the entry-way the peculiar clicking of *babouches* which heralds the approach of a native. A man's voice calls out, " Passage-way? "

Batoul answered, " Pass."

At the same time she left her loom and went to crouch in a corner of the room. A man crossed the patio. He was dressed in a pink *djellaba* over a canary-colored *caftan* ; about his forehead a gold-striped turban was wound in heavy folds. He passed inside the next *koubbas*. He was the husband of one of her neighbors.

Batoul came back to crouch before her loom ; she took up her work once more. Just as she takes up the strands of wool, she resumes the thread of her narrative.

" As a usual thing the maiden does not sleep with her parents. She has her own room. When the *kaouada* comes anew to speak to her, she answers,

" ' Say to Si-Mohamed that he should come on such and such a day, at midnight. I will be behind the door. He only needs to say his name and I will open to him.'

" Matters pass as has been arranged — Lella Fatma lets Si-Mohamed into her room."

" Into her room? — But if her parents found them out? — "

" It sometimes happens. Then they force the young man to make an offer of marriage and to pay the *sadecq*."

" And if he refuses? "

" He does not refuse, for he would be haled before the *cadi* who would sentence him to marry the girl anyway. The *chraa* is legal."

" So, then, the young girl is married ; her marriage does not restore to her the affection and respect of her relatives and friends. Her father, whom she has so deeply offended, takes oath not to see her again and forbids her to appear before him. Think of that! — She has shamed her whole family. The other kinspeople feel the same."

" But, Batoul, at least her husband makes her happy? "

" How could it be? The young man himself has been in difficulties with his own people ; they have covered him with reproaches. He blames his wife ; he picks a quarrel with her. The woman laments,

" ' What thou doest is a wicked thing. It was thee that lured me to sin. Because of thee I am in discord with my people. Because of thee I have lost their affection. Why did I ever listen to thee? — '

" ' Thou wert only too glad to listen to me. How many hadst thou listened to before me!'

" Anger throws pepper on their tongues. They come to insults, blows. One day among many he says the irrevocable words,

[51]

" ' I divorce thee. Pack up thy clothes.' "

" What becomes of her? "

" She returns to her parents ; they take her in to keep her from further adventures ; but for her, happiness is dead. She gets only just enough food to keep her from starving ; no one speaks to her, no one accords her even the least little mark of affection. Never a new *caftan*, a *sebenia* or *kohl*. . . . She is treated worse than the least of the slaves. If her parents are rich enough they hunt a husband for her. Since the sin she committed is known about, they are not so particular. The suitor says, ' I do not intend to pay the *sadecq*.'

" The parents say, ' Thou wilt not have to pay it. We give her to thee for nothing.'

" They break the news to their daughter. She is glad to leave them, to begin a new life ; but to be taken for nothing, to feel that everybody knows it — Allah, Allah, what shame ! "

.   .   .   .

The misconduct of the girl sometimes does not end so favorably as this. The step that she has taken is so grave that in certain families, even to-day, it is considered expiable only by blood. The guilty must disappear.

" Her father, or lacking that, her brother, says to her the simple phrase, ' To-morrow we will make an expedition to the country.'

" She knows what fearful meaning for her is hidden in these apparently friendly words. As soon as they are alone in the *bled* the stock of a revolver will be pressed against her temple ; a knife will slash her throat. Her body will be thrown into a ditch behind the bushes and *chacals* will clean her bones.

" Yet she makes no attempt to avoid her punishment, she will not try to escape ; she bows her head and answers,

" ' *Ourrah*.' (Certainly.)

" She follows the one who leads her away without trying to soften him by her tears. ' Allah has written it over her.' Hers is the dumbness of sheep led to slaughter.

.   .   .   .

In the room opposite that of Batoul, a woman is beginning to prepare the evening meal. Kneeling before an earthen *kanoun* she stirs the simmering *tagine* with a long wooden spoon. She is an old woman, a negress, with a sunken flabby face whose fine glistening color has long since become grayed and dull.

Night falls upon the little patio whose four walls close in as though to choke it.

Batoul has left her work. Soon she will partake of a little *couscus* and then lie down to save candles or oil.

I get up. From the threshold of the room Batoul watches me leave. Her half-bent arm moves in farewell and it is really a farewell that we exchange.

Perhaps never again will I see her poor room, her little patio without a tree, without a fountain to murmur, where nothing would mark the passing seasons if summer did not shed down heat like an oven.

THE VENGEANCE OF FATIMA

CHAPTER V

THE VENGEANCE OF FATIMA

This is the story of what occurred in the house of a Frenchman living in Marrakech.

For several years a youth named Mohamed had been in his employ. This Mohamed's rather striking beauty was always enhanced by his dashing attire — small pink vest entirely braided, purple *gandourahs*, orange *serouals*.

Mohamed was perfectly happy with his master. He never troubled to think, " If my *seroual* were of pistachio green it would be more becoming to my peculiar style, if my vest were of silk it would be more elegant." He never said to himself, " My share of *couscus* might be bigger and my bowl of *harira* deeper " — Satisfied with the lot Allah had donated him, he went about his tasks with a simple and satisfied heart.

But it came about that his master, needing an extra hand in the house, engaged a young maidservant. The charms of this particular girl did not leave the manly Mohamed untroubled. Passing Fatima in the patio, he made soft eyes at her, meeting her in the corridor he tenderly murmured, " Thou art beautiful! I love thee. . . ."

But Fatima would merely pretend that she had not heard, or had not understood, and would run off from him, laughing.

One " day of days " Mohamed beguilingly offered her a silver bracelet. The gift was of no real value, but it tempted the girl — she accepted it.

What was bound to happen, happened. It came to the master's ears.

One morning, standing at the threshold of his room whose doors, painted in rosettes and arabesques, opened on the patio, he clapped his hands sternly twice, " Mohamed! Mohamed! "

Then when his servant stood before him, " Listen well. The Prophet has commanded the Faithful to act according to the dictates of justice in all things. You love this girl Fatima and have proven it to her. Now you must marry her."

The master spoke with the voice of authority, strong in the feeling of accomplishing his duty, but Mohamed cried out indignantly, drawn to his full slim height,

" I, *sidi?* Marry Fatima! Why, it's impossible. I am free-born — and she! — It's enough to look at the color of her skin."

His master did not press the point ; he had no right to insist, but his brows glowered. He foresaw trouble in his household — lover's scorching quarrels, scenes of jealousy. He said,

" Does Fatima know your intention? "

" She does, *sidi.*"

" What does she think of it? "

" Ia, *sidi*, what would you expect her to think? — She's a good girl. She understands so well that I have no intention of marrying her, that she's consented to pick me out another wife. I said to her, ' I want one young and pretty.' — She'll find her, if it be the will of God."

" If it be the will of God," approved the master.

Some time passed after this. The discarded sweetheart showed no rancor toward her erstwhile lover. But she was noticed to go out into the streets more often. She took the slightest pretext to leave the house.

One evening she returned with a shining face.

" Mohamed, I have found the perfect wife for thee."

" Thou knowest her? "

" She is one of my own friends."

" Is she young? "

" She is young."

" Beautiful? "

" Rest easy, thine will be a happy household."

Young Mohamed's heart beat with warm anticipation. " *Inch Allah !* " he cried.

" *Inch Allah !* Now when dost thou wish to marry her? "

Mohamed made a lofty gesture. " I want no marriage such as that of *meskines* — I want a festival like that of *tajers*. That's going to cost me a lot of *flouss*. I'll get married when I've saved up the money."

It took proud Mohamed two full years to amass his fourteen hundred francs.

Then came the announcement of his grand marriage ; the feasts commenced and lasted seven crowded days.

The master, who had become very fond of Mohamed and wished to keep him in his service, offered to contribute toward the wedding expenses. By his generosity Mohamed made his appearance clad in robes of white wool, his dark hair dressed and perfumed. The great hall of the dwelling was decorated with the best rugs and provided with mattresses and soft cushions. Seated on a high chair illuminated in arabesques of vivid colors — the honor seat of the groom — Mohamed carried himself gravely, silently, the hood of his *djellaba* lowered over his thoughtful brow.

At his side the two men-of-honor, the minister and his lieutenant, received on a large tray the wedding presents of the friends who filed past, calling out, " I offer this gift in Allah's name. May he bestow on thee happiness and health ! "

When the moment arrived to conduct young Mohamed to his dwelling, the whole procession started off to the joyful sound of flutes. The groom, his new *babouches* immaculate in the wide white stirrups of a snowy horse, clad from tip to toe in pure white himself, looked like a young prince of the time of the grand caliphs.

Meantime in the wide gardens, songs and dances, perfumes and the prescribed libations rejoiced the hearts of the lucky guests.

When the festivals were over, Mohamed reappeared in his master's service. He had put away his fine holiday raiment and donned his usual working clothes. The other domestics surrounded him with gay greetings but he barely responded to them and left them to go inside. " What's the matter with him? " his fellows asked each other, " he seems so downcast — he looks like a death's head. The true face of a penitent at ˋRamadan ! — And Fatima — where's she hiding herself? "

" She's mad."

[59]

" Why should she be? — Isn't she the one that arranged the match and even chose the bride for Mohamed? " . . .

As soon as his master got out of bed the broken-spirited Mohamed hastened to him.

" *Sidi*, I have something to tell thee. — I want to 'tear up the card' (break the marriage contract)."

" ' Tear up the card? ' Are you crazy? — You've only been married seven days ! "

" *Sidi*, I could manage it easily ; the marriage has never been consummated."

His master made a gesture of stern surprise.

Mohamed cried out, " *Ia*, my master, thou knowest how deceitful women are ! — That Fatima is a dog. Thou rememberest what she said of the wife she had picked out for me, ' She is young and perfectly beautiful ' ?

" Listen, *sidi*, what she did. When I came up to the *arousa* and lifted her veil — I saw a woman so old that she might have been my grandmother's grandmother. Her hair was like matted wool, her eyes were running, her mouth dripping — she was half paralyzed — "

At that instant, and although there was no wind, a drapery hanging at the far end of the room trembled slightly and if Mohamed had not been so absorbed in the recital of his dire misfortune, he might have heard a mocking chuckle.

He continued, " Not to spoil my guest's pleasure, I said nothing. The feasts went on as they ought, but yesterday I found the *cadi* and I told him just what Fatima had done."

" And what was his advice ? "

" This, simply, — Snatch out the tongue that lied to thee — pierce the eyes that saw the truth and then deceived thee ! "

From behind the curtain came a whispered cry of terror. Later, they called in vain for Fatima. Beyond a doubt she had thought it expedient to put some distance between her and a young man who had been given legal advice to carry out so dire, if so just, a punishment.

"ASLEEP IN THE BOSOM OF ITS MOTHER"

CHAPTER VI

"ASLEEP IN THE BOSOM OF ITS MOTHER"

Cherif Moulay-Ibrahim has two wives. They live together; their *koubbas* face each other in his patio.

Could this be because they come originally from the same province, Chaouia? Or because they have the same tattooing?—small blue points at the base of the nose that wash off in the weekly bath, other blue points on the chin that are indelible. Anyway, they resemble each other to me; their dark skins have the same golden glints; their mouths are heavy and full-lipped, their faces moon-shaped. They are considered beauties among their own people.

For those who have never been to Morocco I hasten to add that Lella Toma and her co-wife Lella Zeïneb are not dressed like odalisques in filmy scarfs that reveal each movement of the body. If such visions exist in the Occident it is the fault of various painters and romancers. The reality is quite another thing. In spite of a fiery sun, Morocco is a cold country; there are no fireplaces in native homes, and a bizarre custom decrees that a woman of rank may not warm herself. That would be "shameful." Then how can she keep warm except by adding more garments and making them of cloth and velvet? Falling in unbroken folds to the feet, the stiff, heavy *caftan* has a beauty, a nobility, even a style about it that must be admitted and that makes frills and flounces seem contemptible and a bit ridiculous beside it.

Legs tucked dextrously beneath them, Lella Toma and her companion are sitting side by side on the same mattress. A horror of a carpet spreads its shrieking colors along the floor; there are no *haïtis* (hangings) on the walls; the mattresses are covered by a simple cretonne. My hostesses are *cherifas* and follow the *Maghzen* tradition. Not in their houses may you lounge on silks and satins.

[63]

Just now in bidding me welcome, the two wives lavished upon me all the formulas of politeness,

"Be thou welcome! — *Baraka* (fortune) visits us with thy presence!"

Now they curiously examine the fashions of Europe as they appear on my person. They explain for my benefit that they love each other like sisters — seldom do they ever quarrel. They assert, proudly: "In all Marrakech you will not find a household like ours."

"Last summer," says Lella Zeïneb, "I nearly died. Lella Toma nursed me like my own mother. Never will I forget it."

Lella Toma will not forget it either, perhaps. But Allah — what is she doing? She bends toward her co-wife, seizes her by the throat, her fingers clench.

"This one," she mutters, "I ought to strangle her — she has taken my husband!"

They both burst into long laughing. Lella Toma, who is demonstrative, slaps her thighs. It was only a joke. A "Morocco" joke. But all the same, if these two women did not love each other so much . . .

Under a "gazelle-blood" colored *caftan* which the *ferragiat* veils, Lella Zeïneb displays, not without ostentation, a pregnancy near its end. All the favors of the master are hers. Lella Zeïneb is young.

Beside her Lella Toma looks like a large sack tied in the middle. She is still "mistress of things" and orders the household, but she is displaced. She pretends not to notice the humiliation.

Generously she remarks, "Lella Zeïneb, thou seest, has a 'round womb'; she has already had five children."

"And you?"

"I have three and will have no more. I have one asleep now in my bosom."

"You?"

"By Allah I swear it. He has been sleeping ever since the French arrived. He got frightened then and would not appear. Many other women in Marrakech are in the same condition."

The arrival of the French in the city? — That goes back to 1912. Lella Toma's child has been sleeping for fifteen years!

[64]

It seems that it tires her to carry it. She has pains in her back and hips. She begs me,

" Give me a *doue* to waken him, wilt thou not? "

" You must ask one from the *toubeba* (medicine woman)."

" She says she has nothing for that."

" Neither have I."

" Oh my fathers, must my child dry up and turn into a stick? "

She breaks into loud lamentations. Happy Lella Zeïneb, who has no sleeping child and soon will be a mother again, throws her a pitying glance.

" *Meskina, meskina*," she murmurs sincerely.

The click of a pair of *babouches* sounds on the flag-stones of the entry. The children who were playing in the patio hush their noise, the women have lowered their voices. The doorway frames the massive figure of Moulay-Ibrahim and his golden yellow turban.

" Greeting," he bows to me. " May the morning give you joy."

" Greeting."

" So thou art again amongst us? "

" I love Marrakech."

" Thou art right. Yet may I ask why thou preferrest our city? "

" There is such a clear light here, the mountains are so beautiful. . . ."

The Marrakechi's grave eyes glow with pleasure. Seating himself tailor-fashion, leaning comfortably against the cushions, he adds,

" Those things that have struck thee here, Allah himself commands us to admire. In a true Moslem the sentiment of beauty is united to religious feeling. Hast thou read the Koran? Then thou knowest the verses where, speaking to the Arabs who live only in tents, God tells them,

" ' Must one not admire the manner in which the camels are fashioned, the way the sky domes above the earth, the way the mountains have been set each in its place, and the way the earth elsewhere has been planned? ' "

. . . .

Lella Toma and Lella Zeïneb have left us to look after their household affairs. The children have vanished. Careful of his duties as

[67]

host Moulay-Ibrahim notices that I have only one cushion to rest on. He gets up, collects all those scattered on the mattress, arranges them at my back and under my arms, then, satisfied with the soft nook he has made for me, he bends courteously low.

" The sultana's corner," says he.

Back in his own corner he lights a cigarette. He smokes in a droll manner which I have only seen in him. Head thrown back, he holds his cigarette vertically, blowing very straight puffs that made a sound like " fff, fff, fff, fff. . . ."

Except for that there is silence. The Moroccans have not the same ideas as ours about social duties. They do not feel themselves obliged to entertain their visitors continually. If someone wants to talk, he talks ; if he prefers to be still, they leave him to his silence. What a relief! What rest!

My eyes are half closed and I am lost in day-dreaming. As an amusement which I often allow myself, and which is like going to a costume ball, I am no longer *Roumiya* but Moorish ; this is my house ; I have on a *caftan* of " bishop-purple " velvet like that of fat Lella Toma, with a wide and heavy girdle of embroidery. My feet are shod in shimmering gilt *babouches*, a tight-fitting silken kerchief swathes my head. Until my death, only at rare intervals will I leave these walls that close me in. In order to think as they do, I try to recall the confidences of certain native women. When I have condoled with them for living like recluses, they responded,

" It is thou that dost not know true happiness. No Western wife is so loaded with favors as the least of us. For our husbands each feast is an excuse for offering us a trinket, a veil or a *caftan* of the latest shade."

" That may be, but your lives are without security ; your husbands have the right to divorce you any moment — they have only to say a word. Only their wishes count."

" Unless he is insane what husband would discard his wife without grave reasons? "

" But if such should come up? "

" The wife is no less happy for that. She is divorced, she remarries again. . . ."

I recall other confidences. Confidences of husbands. They say,

" When a quarrel breaks out it is not always the husband who gets the upper hand. Does he make a comment? The wife flies into a passion. Does he answer back? She shouts all the louder. Does he refuse to answer? She takes that for a reason to heap abuse upon him. Finally there is only one thing left to do — to take up his *djellaba*, his cane, and walk off, saying, ' One does not quarrel with Satan. . . .'

This he does. He goes to the *souks*, the *fondouks*, the café. Struck by his haggard mien, his friends question him,

" What is the matter? Are you sick? "

At first he says nothing but at last he admits,

" Satan, the accursed, has thrown discord into my house."

His friends comfort him, " Is that all? We have all been through that. It will come out all right."

The husband responds, " *Inch Allah!* " and takes himself home.

Talking with his friends, changing scenes, has soothed him. On her side, the wife has been calmed by her negresses. Peace reigns until the next quarrel.

It might be objected, " But there are others of more vindictive natures. . . ."

Quite right. In such a case, and when the woman who feels herself offended is not above teaching her husband a lesson, she will say,

" All is ended. I am insulted! "

With that she leaves him and goes back to her parents.

Then it is all the worse for the husband. Everything in the house goes wrong. Like good and devoted slaves the negresses have taken their mistress' part. No matter how much the husband shouts they pay no attention to him. His *couscus* is burned, his *tagines* are cold ; there is no hot water for his ablutions, no tea. Can one call that living? For a time, out of pure self-respect, he holds out, but the day comes when he seeks his parents-in-law's home. Behind the half-opened door the wife hears him lavishing promises and protestations. One can't hold anger forever. . . .

Her conditions made, the triumphant wife returns to her husband's

roof and the reconciliation is celebrated by a reunion of relatives and friends.
. . . .

Before me the patio of Moulay-Ibrahim shimmers softly in all its bluish tiles. Its wide archways frame the azure sky.

Fatima is strolling along the tile-paved, cloister-like walk that encircles the courtyard. She is a rather buxom mulatto, but young and healthy as befits the slave of an honorable and well-tended household. When she reaches the threshold of the room where we sit, she takes up her master's *babouches*, turns them toes out so they will be easy to slip into. Drawing herself up again, she rests a lazy shoulder on the lintel of the door. At a sign from Moulay-Ibrahim she moves on off, swaying herself, unhurried, curious, fascinated. Her firm, dark body has a robust sort of beauty. A green *caftan*, looped high over her black cloth *seroul*, forms a queer tail down her back like a chicken's.

Lounging comfortably against his cushions, his dark face in repose, Moulay-Ibrahim lights a fresh cigarette. What if I should ask him about the old belief of " children asleep in the bosom of their mother "? He would be better able than anyone to answer me. He studied for seven years at the University at Karouyne and, as if Allah had set him in my path to instruct me exactly, it happens that years ago he was a *cadi* somewhere on the *bled*.

Contrary to my expectation, Moulay-Ibrahim does not smile at my question. In his fine and intelligent countenance, his eyes, which always squint a trifle, only close tighter — a sign in him of attention. In his extraordinarily soft voice, he makes a grave reply,

" The belief of infants asleep in their mother's womb is recognized by the *chraa*."

" But, *cadi*, the intelligence refuses — "

" Listen ; I will tell thee one of our theological laws ; ' Intelligence only corroborates. It is not the principle. That is God.' Dost admit that God has the right to preside over the continuation of life? "

" The question is superfluous."

" Dost also admit that the intelligence is limited? There are gaps — it believes that it knows all and therefore ignores."

[70]

" Undoubtedly."

" Since we are agreed, then, let us leave generalities. Let us suppose that I am still a *cadi*. A woman comes to me. Her husband has divorced her. She tells me, ' For twelve months I have been with child.' She has all the signs that confirm her statement. Intelligence has a right to protest, to declare, ' What this woman says is impossible '; but the Divine Principle speaks louder and proclaims, ' I remind thee that thou, Intelligence, knowest nothing and art subject to deception.'

" Applying the laws of the *chraa*, I impose a waiting time of nine months on the woman. I say to her, ' During those nine months I forbid thee to marry again. It would be a sin for the corn to be harvested by him who has not sown it.' Midwives designated by me visit and keep watch over the woman. The child does not enter the world. Three times further delays of nine months are imposed on the mother. The child continues to sleep. I have the woman brought before me.

" ' What news hast thou? '

" ' None. I still feel the child. It moves and struggles.'

" Although forty-eight months have passed already, I believe with the woman that she bears a sleeping child and I decree,

" Thou must undergo a further waiting of nine months and remember that during that time I forbid thee to remarry."

" She agrees, ' Very well, *cadi*.'

" The nine months pass. The child is not born. What now? I call a physician and inquire of the midwives instructed to watch over the woman. The doctor says,

" ' A woman is not an elephant. She does not carry her child for fifty-seven months.'

" The midwives persist in their statement. ' There is a child and it is sleeping.' "

In order to light a fresh cigarette, Moulay-Ibrahim is silent for a moment; then he demands,

" If thou hadst been in my place what wouldst thou have believed? "

" I would believe the doctor."

" Very well — but I believed the midwives. They are women and in this question they know better than any man how a woman feels. I impose on the young mother a further waiting of twenty-seven months."

" *Cadi, cadi,* you are exaggerating! "

" It is the law. These delays over, I, the *cadi,* speak in thought to the sleeping child, ' Well, why art thou waiting to appear? ' — Why dost smile? "

By his suddenly changed tone I guess that it is to me my host is speaking. Oh yes, I had smiled. There was something in his way of interrogating the tiny life, in so little hurry to be born, — an air of naïveté, of simplicity which amused me infinitely and piqued my curiosity. What was the baby going to answer? Something very infantile, no doubt. But Moulay-Ibrahim insists that I am mistaken.

" No, listen : The child says, ' What tells thee that I must be born at the end of twenty-four months? Thou knowest by experience that I can live after six months, but how dost thou know at the end of what time Allah has willed me to awaken? '

" Having heard this," says Moulay-Ibrahim, " I impose further delays upon the woman."

" *Cadis* are there for that! — "

" I say to her, ' Wait twenty-four more months.' "

" Poor woman! "

" Do not pity her. Her patience is exhausted. She has married again. A child is born."

" Allah be praised! The little sleeper awakens! "

" He wakens, but our troubles are not ended yet. There are two possibilities."

" Only two? Incredible."

" Either the child is born within six months after the mother remarries, or he is born afterward. Let us say that he is born within the six months. The first husband presents himself. Everyone is assembled around the new-born. The physician is confounded, the midwives are triumphant. The first husband demands,

" ' Is the child alive? '

" They answer, ' It is.'

" Upon which the husband replies, ' It is mine. I will take it. My wife was carrying this child when I divorced her; she has never ceased to carry it; the child was asleep; it is mine.' "

" Moulay-Ibrahim, do you want to know what I am going to say? — I have the greatest admiration for that husband."

My host smiles back in his black beard.

" Thou art right, because it is rare in these times that one finds such a chance. A life is valuable — A child — "

.   .   .   .

In one of the corridors of the dwelling a furious voice broke out, " Off-spring of a renegade! Dog! — "

Lella Toma appeared. Rages inflated her; it seemed that during the half hour since she had left us she had found means of puffing up still more. She marched up to her husband.

" Ya, *sidi!* That girl Fatima! Listen — a beggar was crying at the door. I sent her two *pesetas* by Fatima — she kept one for her-self — "

Due to my presence, Moulay-Ibrahim pretended not to hear, but after a moment he got up. I was left with Lella Toma whose indigna-tion continued to mount. She mixed its terms with abuse for Fatima and her insults were as numerous as the sands of the desert.

" To steal from a beggar! That Fatima is worse than any dog. Oh my master, weep for her because I will not open to her. I would let her die of hunger before I would give her to eat! May Allah strike her blind or kill her with cholera! "

From the depths of the house sounded a groan and then another, and then another still. At the same moment as I and even sooner, Lella Toma also heard it. The habit of living in a house nearly always silent gives a very subtle hearing to native women. She left the mattress on which she was sitting; I saw her disappear inside.

For a moment I waited her return. And then — well, curiosity overpowered me. I, too, slipped into the corridor where my hosts were engaged. As I advanced the groans, the outcries grew louder.

" Allah! Allah! Not so hard! He is killing me! Allah save me — "

In a little patio, onto which opens the narrow and smoky room that

[73]

serves as a kitchen, the slave Fatima had been thrown on the floor. Moulay-Ibrahim was beating her with a leather strap. It rose and fell regularly. Between strokes the slave cried out,

"Enough! Enough! It was devils entered my head! The mercy of Allah! Mercy!"

The children of the house formed a semicircle. They looked on at the performance as at a play. They looked as eagerly as when the serpent-charmer or the fire-eater performs in the square Djemaa el F'na.

Judging the punishment sufficient, Moulay-Ibrahim threw away his whip. The beating had made him warm. He raised his turban and rapidly passed his hand over his shaven head.

Fatima had taken refuge in the kitchen. Her negro face was swollen and ashine.

"Allah, Allah!" she continued to whimper. "I had devils in my head. They possessed me — "

Slowly she draped her *caftan* again and reknotted her *sebenia* which had slipped from her forehead and given a glimpse of the dark mass of her hair divided into little plaits as hard as cords.

Her mistress and the children looked on as well as the other slave. With a sort of pride one of the little boys noted, "He flailed her long enough to recite two chaplets."

Her complaints move no one to pity. When she had rearranged her clothes, Fatima disappeared inside the kitchen. Lella Toma's contemptuous voice pursued her,

"Shameful girl! Let this teach thee to steal from the poor!"

AN ESCAPE FROM THE HAREM

CHAPTER VII

AN ESCAPE FROM THE HAREM

Slavery is banned in Morocco. Sincere and enlightened Moroccans themselves admit that slavery as it is practiced to-day is contrary not only to civil law but, which is far more important in their sight, to religious law. And yet there is scarcely a native household where one or more slaves are not found. As a rule they are well treated. Well nourished, seldom overworked, they automatically become like members of the family. As Lella Toma remarked to me after Fatima's punishment, " A good slave is never beaten." Those who " eat of the stick " deserve it. In the tone we would use to say, "What a nuisance servants are!", she concluded, " If you only knew how exasperating a slave can be!"

Lella Toma is right about the majority of slaves. Those who fall to merciful and humane masters are numerous, but there are always exceptions. Let me cite one of them.

A certain Mme. Dumont has lived in Fez for the past ten years. She is a widow and lives a very retired life. Her house, situated in the Medina, adjoins that of a notable to whom Allah has accorded considerable fortune. As is usual in a Moslem country, this fortune is manifested by the possession of numerous slaves. El Hadj Mohamed uses a great many of them. He mistreats them out of cruelty ; he undernourishes them out of stinginess.

From time to time some among them try to run away. Escape is not easy from one roof top to another, but with luck there is a possibility of success.

One night Mme. Dumont's sleep was troubled by loud outcries. She listened. The groans came from El Hadj Mohamed's house. Mme. Dumont thought that one of her neighbor's wives must be ill and went back to sleep ; but the night following the same cries were heard.   They were so poignant that the Frenchwoman was deeply troubled.   Determined to find out who was shrieking, she mounted the stairs to her roof.

To understand what follows, it must be explained that Mme. Dumont's house overlooks the neighboring roof.   Dawn had not yet lifted. The moon was darkened by little round scudding clouds, a cold wind made her shiver.   Mme. Dumont leaned over the parapet of her roof but saw nothing.   The massed clouds thinned ; the moon rode out.

In the center of the rectangular space of a patio forming part of El Hadj Mohamed's dwelling grew one of those trees which the natives, because of their numerous big round berries, commonly call chapelet trees.   A white form was perched up in it.

It could just be seen in the twilight like a poor, shivering bird huddling in the midst of the branches.

At the sight of the Frenchwoman the form waved its arms and its cries redoubled.   Mme. Dumont knew little Arabic.   She only confusedly understood a few words of the appeals addressed to her.   She went down and called her servant Brika.

Having sworn her to secrecy as to what she was to see and hear, Mme. Dumont led her up to the roof.   Dawn began to break.   Night birds still swooped about in the sky.   Each house was silent as a tomb. Pathos ascended from the sleeping gray city and gripped the heart.

Huddled in a fork formed by two branches, the white human figure still whimpered softly.   On hearing the two women she turned her face toward them and hushed crying.

" Who art thou and what art thou doing in the patio? " demanded Brika.

Half in *chleuh* and half in Arabic the confiding answer came back,

" Oh my mother, I am Johra, one of the slaves of El Hadj Mohamed. I broke one of the tea glasses and the boiling tea fell on my *sidi's* feet. He beat me so hard that my back is striped.   I tried to run away but the doorkeeper brought me back.   Then my *sidi* ordered them to shut me out in this patio."

" But why didst thou climb into the tree? "

" Oh my master, I am so afraid out here by myself.   I climbed up

[78]

to see if some one in the next houses might not hear me. I did right —
Thou and the Nazarene have come. I am so hungry! They only threw
me a crumb of *kessera* this morning. My mouth is as parched as the
oued in summer. The porter forgets to bring me water — "

Word by word, Mme. Dumont got Brika to translate what she had
heard. Her heart burned with pity.

"Tell that child to take courage," she said. "I am going to try to
save her."

When they climbed down, the Frenchwoman threw herself on a couch.
It was still too early to do anything and she wished to think. The image
of that unhappy child, trembling with cold and fear in the tree where she
had taken refuge, and tortured with hunger and thirst, took shape in
the courageous woman's mind and became an obsession.

What could she do about it? After long thought, Mme. Dumont
believed she had found a solution.

On several occasions she had employed a native named Kaddour for
various odd jobs. He was an athletic sort of man and quite resourceful.
Having sent for him, Mme. Dumont explained to him what she expected
of him. She spoke in her most moving, persuasive tones. Kaddour
listened in silence.

"What thou askest of me," he said finally, "is impossible. Go
down by the roof into the patio of El Hadj Mohamed? The blessing of
Allah upon thee, but thou wouldst have me shot!"

"No one would see you," returned Mme. Dumont forcefully. "The
patio is at the far end of the house."

"It is at the far end, but the slave fastened up in it is certainly watched.
Behind some convenient door there is a guard. A load of shot, I tell
thee, that's all I'll get, and El Hadj Mohamed would be within his rights
in shooting me. I'd be breaking into his house."

As Kaddour set out his reasons, Mme. Dumont realized more fully
the difficulties of the enterprise into which she intended to throw herself.

Resolved in spite of it to rescue the unhappy Johra, she cried,

"Listen, Kaddour, there will be a *fabor* in it for you. Do you think
two hundred *douros* — "

The hercules' face remained impassive, but under his *chechia*, in the dark of his eyes, a light began to gleam. The vastness of the sum all but blinded him. He lost his breath over it and forgot the dangers to which he would be exposed. Two hundred *douros!* Never had he possessed so much *flouss* at one time in his life. . . .

Mme. Dumont intended to take advantage of this emotion and without giving him a chance to recover himself, she added,

" It is understood, then. I will make the necessary preparations. You are to be here this evening after *Moghreb*."

But by trying to hurry things along too fast, she had risked compromising everything. The man had recovered himself.

" Allah! Allah! This evening! — I must think it over. To-morrow I will return and give thee an answer. . . ."

In the course of the day Mme. Dumont went to the European quarter and there bought a long, stout rope. The attempt at flight was made more difficult in that the patio where she found Johra was separated from her own roof by an open passage. This passageway, which belonged to El Hadj Mohamed, was closed at both ends.

To save the little slave it was necessary not only to get her up over the ten-foot wall enclosing her patio, but after getting her into the passageway, to hoist her up the wall to the neighboring roof. And this stood not less than thirteen feet above the ground. Its masonry was covered with a perfectly smooth plaster — not a projection, not a crack affording foothold or a grip for the hand.

Another night commenced. The Frenchwoman spent it without sleep. Johra's heart-rending cries never left her ears. Tormented by the thought of the rescue she intended to attempt the next day, Mme. Dumont persuaded herself one moment that Kaddour would consent to help her and that all would go smoothly, the next that he would refuse — and then what could she do?

Kaddour kept her waiting the whole morning. Though Mme. Dumont tried hard to delude herself, this belatedness did not augur well. Nor was she mistaken. When at last the man reappeared it was to say,

" The risks are too great. I prefer to keep my skin, myself."

Mme. Dumont heard it in anguish. "Come, Kaddour," she pleaded,

" and you a brave man! It is impossible to leave the poor little thing like this. — Think if it were your own child — "

The words came from her heart, but the big chap was unshaken. " It will only mean one daughter of Eve less," was his comment.

His egotism, his native insensibility, revolted Mme. Dumont. " But she is going to die, to die of hunger. It is criminal! "

The giant looked back unflinching and answered simply, " *Inch Allah* — if it pleases God." His blamelessness in the affair was stated.

He left Mme. Dumont in despair. Outside, as if Johra knew that her life was at stake, her appeals and cries redoubled. Never had they been so moving. To keep from hearing them, the Frenchwoman locked herself in her room ; she pressed her hands to her ears but peace would not come. A terrible certainty mastered her ; if help were not forthcoming now, Johra would surely perish.

Toward the end of the afternoon Mme. Dumont could bear it no longer. She was one of those brave, energetic women whom danger cannot restrain when duty impels them. Later, telling me of the adventures which followed, she said, " I had thought of all the consequences of my action. I knew to what I exposed myself and I was not ignorant of the perils that confronted me. If I had been certain I was going to my death, I would not have turned back."

Toward the hour of *Moghreb* she ascended to her roof. The weather was still cold and the neighboring roofs were deserted. In the fire of a setting sun the pyramidal roofs of the sanctuary of Moulay-Idriss shimmered like emeralds. A lantern was lighted in the minaret of the mosque of Andolous and the white pennon of prayer was unfurled. At the signal, all the other minarets hastened to respond and hoisted their pure white banners. An uninterrupted murmur mounted up from the *souks*.

Mme. Dumont was just about to lean over her parapet. Suddenly her hand was seized and she was drawn violently backward. Brika, her servant, had crouched beside her.

" Allah! " she was whispering, " hide thyself."

Concealed behind the wall they both crept to the other corner and knelt down. They were just in time.

[81]

In the sort of passageway outside the patio where Johra was imprisoned, there was a murmur of voices. Voices speaking in Arabic.

Accompanied by two workmen, El Hadj Mohamed was pretending to inspect the state of the wall whose upkeep fell to him. Had Kaddour let his tongue wag? Had someone in the house of the Fasci spied out Mme. Dumont's unusual comings and goings on her roof? Had she been overheard speaking to Johra? — Plainly El Hadj Mohamed had not come into his passage, had not spoken so loudly nor pretended interest in the state of a wall in perfect condition, except to give his French neighbor to understand that Johra was being watched.

Far from discouraging Mme. Dumont, this thought only served to strengthen her resolution. Difficulties and opposition act as spurs to energetic natures. For reasons of prudence, however, she decided to wait until the latter part of the night before attempting her project. Then it was to be hoped that, worn with watching, the prisoner's unseen guard might be asleep.

Some hours later, Mme. Dumont again climbed the narrow stairway that gave access to the neighboring roofs. Brika, who followed her, carried the coil of rope that had been bought during the afternoon.

The moon had not yet risen but the darkness was not complete. The nights of *Moghreb* are as clear as those of the Orient.

Mme. Dumont directed her steps to the part of the roof that overlooked the patio. Contrary to what had happened during the previous nights, a profound silence, the silence of the grave, reigned above the narrow space. The plaints of the little captive were stilled.

Filled with uneasiness and the worst forebodings, Mme. Dumont called first softly and then in a louder tone to the little slave,

" Johra! Johra! "

Ears strained, she listened with all her senses, tensed for an answer however feeble. Nothing.

What had become of the child? In the tree's indistinguishable branches one could no longer make out the palish glimmer of her dress. A frightful anguish assailed Mme. Dumont. Was Johra already dead? Had she been taken to another, a more secret and horrible prison?

Her heart twisted by terror, the Frenchwoman recalled all that she

[82]

had heard of the inhuman punishments inflicted by cruel masters. She imagined the helpless creature flung into some dark pit. By trying to save her, she had only made her agony worse. . . .

She was in the midst of these imaginings, not knowing where to turn, when her servant Brika tugged her dress.

"Lella," she whispered, "let me try."

By means of a large stone Brika jumped to the coping of the roof, sat on it and leaned far over.

Mme. Dumont did not breathe. What was it Brika hoped to see in the passageway? She did not have long to wait. Brika sprang down from her post of vantage.

"Johra is lying at the foot of our wall. She lies there like some big bundle. She does not move."

"Are you sure it is she?"

"By Allah and the Prophet, I saw her myself."

Guessing by her master's appearance in the passage that her imprisonment was to be made more severe, feeling that her very life was at stake, Johra had made a desperate effort. With strength lent by imminent danger, she had managed to bound from her tree to the top of the wall ; from there she had attempted to slide down. Either clumsiness or weakness had made her fall.

How long could she have been lying there, unconscious or with broken back? — No matter ; the essential thing was to act before her disappearance was reported in the house of El Hadj Mohamed. This meant to raise the fallen body and haul it up to the roof. Would this be possible? Mme. Dumont considered the height of the wall and was dismayed.

"Listen," she said to the servant, "of the two of us you are the lighter. Tie the rope around your waist ; I am going to let you down. When you have picked up Johra, I will pull you both up."

As though it were the most natural thing on earth, Brika accepted without a second's hesitation. A few minutes later she hung spinning at the end of the rope. Careful not to give too much rope and to avoid jars, her mistress let her down.

Everything went as well as could be expected. Arrived on the ground

[83]

of the passage, Brika picked up the child, tied her to the rope and hung on herself.

On the roof top, Mme. Dumont started hauling in.

The passage and the patio were still deserted. In the domain of El Hadj Mohamed the sentries slept on. But Mme. Dumont had not pulled up the double burden many feet before she realized the folly of her attempt. The poor woman was no longer young, her strength threatened to betray her, and worst of all, she realized that she was not of sufficient counter-weight to maintain her balance. The two girls risked pulling her downward.

To fail so near the end! — Rage in her heart, Mme. Dumont braced her arms, bore back on the weight, tautened her muscles. She felt herself growing weaker and no help under heaven at hand. She must do it alone or give it up. Give up? Never that. — The Frenchwoman made a supreme effort. Her slipping foot struck against a heavy stone, the same that Brika had rolled against the parapet to mount on. An idea sprang alive in Mme. Dumont's heart. — Johra might yet be saved.

The stone was tightly fastened at the end of the rope — the counter-weight was established. Again the brave woman began to haul. A quarter of an hour later she pulled her young servant and the body of the little slave over the edge of the roof. The figure was lax but still warm. Mme. Dumont gathered her into her arms. What state was the unhappy child in? In the light of the moon she looked like a skeleton, infested with vermin and covered with sores.

Mme. Dumont bore her to her room. In a short time Johra came to herself; she was lucky enough to have sprained only her wrist in the fall.

Warmed, consoled, it came over her that her agonies were ended. In a glow of childish gratitude she kissed the hem of Mme. Dumont's skirt.

" Oh," she cried, " I love thee like my mother — "

The most perilous part of the escape was accomplished. But Johra had still to be placed in safety, and that before the break of day. There was no doubt but that when El Hahj Mohamed heard of his slave's disappearance, he would set up a search for her. He might even send someone to Mme. Dumont.

She had a French friend at the other end of the city. She resolved to confide the child to her; later on they would see about returning her to her tribe. But it was impossible to send Johra with only Brika as a guide. At the first of the gates that separated the two quarters from each other, the two young creatures would be arrested for night-prowling and sent to the *pasha's* jail.

In spite of her weariness, Mme. Dumont did not hesitate. She covered Johra with a *haik* and wrapped herself in a coat. The heavy gates of the quarters would open freely for a European. The sentry lets them pass without question.

For a long time Mme. Dumont walked the narrow, sloping streets. When she returned dawn was whitening; several of the faithful, their red felt rugs under their arms, were making their way to the mosque for prayer.

Mme. Dumont had done well to hasten. Morning had scarcely commenced when the knocker of her door sounded. Two women presented themselves. They were, they said, vendors of ointments and perfumes. Liars — Brika recognized them immediately as belonging to the household of El Hadj Mohamed.

It would have been easy to turn them away, but Mme. Dumont had no such intention. "Have them come in," she said to her servant, "bring them to my room."

She received them there herself. They were two old crones with wrinkled faces and obsequious manners. They produced essences and unguents, carefully arranged for, from their *haiks*.

"Wilt thou not buy," they cajoled, holding them up. "They are not dear. Look on them for the delight of thy eyes and smell them for that of thy nose."

They stayed above an hour extolling their so-called merchandise. Finally one of them let fall, as though negligently,

"Thy dwelling is large and beautiful to see. Allah has been good to thee; he has given thee all thou couldst desire."

At the same time their inquisitive eyes pried in every corner. After so much anguish Mme. Dumont tasted a vital and malicious joy.

"My dwelling is not large or beautiful," she responded courteously, "if you wish to see it, it is easy to show you over it."

[85]

They roamed from room to room.

"Never," she told me, "shall I forget the crestfallen look of these two women when, after having been through all the rooms, they were compelled to admit that the one they searched for was there no longer. . . ."

FAIR AÏCHA

CHAPTER VIII

FAIR AÏCHA

Following such a tragic tale, it is fitting to give one of a vastly different character. Both are exceptional, but both hold a certain interest as human documents.

Such as it is, the one I am about to tell took place in Rabat. I have seen the heroine myself in one of the *ayals*. And as for the hero, anyone may meet him in the streets.

Si Ahmed ben Omar was in the habit of making a daily visit to one of his friends, Si Ibrahim ben Lhassen. He went after the *acha*, which is the last of the five prayers to be recited by believers. The two young men, who had very decided tastes for poetry, amused themselves by declaiming to each other the verses they had composed. Each in his heart believed his own superior to the other's, but with great courtesy said the opposite, and their friendship, because of it, knew no clouds.

The evening of which I speak passed at first exactly like those that had preceded it. It was not until later that Si Ahmed understood that on this particular day, one hour of his life had been singled out by Allah from amongst all the other hours.

The two friends had finished picking in the white pyramid of *couscus* which constitutes the evening meal of most households ; the basin and ewer for the ablutions had been brought in. Si Ibrahim struck his palms together three times, lightly, as becomes a gentleman of breeding.

Then occurred the event, the very small event, whose ends Allah alone comprehended.

A slave appeared bearing the tray for the tea. Glancing at her mechanically, Ahmed realized that she was new in the house and of unequalled beauty. Slender as the cypress tree, she was yet more graceful than the gazelle, whose caressing glance was hers. Her skin, white as the jasmin-flower, showed that she was free-born.

Attentive to her duties, eyelids lowered, three times she made the gesture of presenting to Si Ahmed and to her master the crystal glasses with golden arabesques that contained the mint-flavored tea. Each time in taking the glass that was intended for him, Si Ahmed caught himself murmuring, " *Barak Allah ou fik.*" (The blessing of Allah upon thee.)

With the wide copper tray balanced on her five fingers spread fan-wise, the girl disappeared across the patio.

Lounging as usual on the mattress, the two friends watched her withdraw. Ibrahim said simply, sure that Si Ahmed would under-stand,

" Caïd Omar of Oulad-Saïd brought her yesterday and left her for me as a gift. Her name is Aïcha."

" Caïd Omar is a true Baramiki — his gift is worthy of a sultan."

Nothing more was said. Si Ibrahim drew a pad from his *caftan* and opening its leaves,

" Hear the verses which I composed while awaiting thee."

> " The cheeks of her I love are more rose-like
> than roses in the sultan's borders.
>
> The eyes of my beloved are darker
> than the hard ebon wood.
>
> Glimmering brighter than the diamond,
> the locks of my beloved. . . ."

The hours passed. A little before midnight, Ibrahim got up and disappeared in the passageway leading to the *ayal*. Among themselves the two friends were accustomed to acting so freely that Si Ahmed felt no surprise at being left alone. At the end of a very short time, however, Ibrahim reappeared and accompanied his guest to the door which opened onto the street. Near the threshold, beside the stone bench reserved for the gate-keeper and for visitors, a woman waited. She stood motionless, enveloped in the whiteness of her *haik*. Nothing of her face was visible except the glinting line of her eyes ; beneath the thick folds of stuff one would judge her to be young and slender.

With a glance Ibrahim designated her to his friend.

" She pleased thee — take her. I give her to thee."

Ahmed bowed deeply. " The blessing of Allah be upon thee — "

Babouches clicking on earth hardened by weeks after weeks of drought, Ahmed and Aïcha, one following the other, disappeared in a turn of the street. There floated only a slender crescent of moon in the sky, but the stars shone countless and with so pure a light that even the narrowest streets were shadowless. An even, lifeless light radiated from the long white walls that surrounded them on either side.

As he walked along Si Ahmed mused on this beautiful girl who had been given him, who followed him and who was at his mercy as master.

A strange sensation, a sensation never before experienced, possessed him. This Aïcha who was his slave — he knew himself incapable of treating her as such.

At the end of a silent street, they reached his house. The door-keeper was stretched out on guard under the arch of the doorway. He was an old man, astonishingly hairy and misshapen. He had seen Ahmed born, had held him in his arms, and when he spoke to him he had the look of a faithful dog in his shaggy eyes.

Si Ahmed said a few words to him. The porter led Aïcha to the women's quarters and the young master went alone to his room.

After the third prayer the next day, he sent for Aïcha. In a red *caftan* whose brilliance was softened by the veiling *ferragiat*, the girl seemed even more alluring than at evening. Ahmed asked her,

" Whence camest thou? "

She named a hamlet between Agadir and Taroudant, in the Sous.

" How camest thou here? "

" Allah willed it."

" He is the all-powerful. Tell me how it came about."

" My father is a caravan leader. Each Tuesday he leads his camels to Agadir to the *souks*. My mother, my sister and I stayed at home alone. Some weeks ago, in the night of Tuesday or Wednesday, two men broke into our house. They gagged and bound my mother; they led me and my sister, who is younger than I, away. They sold us to a dealer in slaves. I was already betrothed. The marriage feast was to be celebrated after the *Ait-el-Kebir*."

These words, though they filled Si Ahmed with deep pity, were not without causing him grave displeasure. During the night he had come to a decision not to keep Aïcha but to marry her off to some honorable man. The realization of this project became impossible. First, because in a Moslem country the father — or failing a father, the guardian — alone has the right to give a young girl in marriage; second, because she was already betrothed. The betrothal is binding among Moslems, constituting a formal contract. It equals the marriage itself; the rights which it confers on the young girl are such that, if the fiancé dies, she inherits from him.

Si Ahmed fell into deep thought. He wanted above all things to be just.

On the next day he sent for two *adouls* (notaries) and before them signed an act liberating his new slave; then he wrote to her parents. He explained to them the circumstances through which Aïcha came to be in his house and enjoined them to come for her as soon as they could.

It is far from Rabat to the land of Tarouedant and for Moroccans the notion of time exists no more forcefully than a care for the future. Everything considered, it is perhaps in these two particulars that Mahometans differ most from Westerners.

Several weeks went by. By Si Ahmed's orders Aïcha was not treated as a slave. She was exempt from all heavy work. She spent her days before her loom, weaving. She appeared in her master's room only to serve his tea. He never addressed her, he avoided looking at her, but when he was alone and unable to sleep, it was not the apparition of a *djena* that he feared, and against which his old *dada* tried to preserve him by placing a bowl filled with water near his door — it was the image of Aïcha.

Absent, she stood alive before his tired eyes; the room seemed to glimmer with the radiance of her white face.

Aïcha had already had time to weave three quarters of a great *burnous* of fine white wool, when one morning she heard her master call her name.

She left the women's apartment, crossed the patio and stood at the threshold of the room where Ahmed was. A rugged desert man stood beside him. His feet were bare. He wore only a dust-covered *gandourah* which stopped above his knees ; around his head was wound a camel's-hair *rezza*.

" Approach, Aïcha," Ahmed said. " Thy father is ailing, thy mother too old to travel, I hear. They have sent thy cousin Hassan to fetch thee back to them. Go, prepare thy clothing."

But Aïcha shook her head.

" If it were my father or my mother or my betrothed who had come to fetch me, I would have gone. I recognize Hassan, but I refuse to follow him. It is unfitting for a young girl and against her honor to travel alone with a cousin."

She stood there, speaking calmly. Si Ahmed could only find that her judgment was sane, her heart pure, and that she was evidently the daughter of people respectful of the *caïda*.

" Thou art right," he said.

Hassan returned alone to the country of Taroudant where the olive trees thrive, and Aïcha went back to the weaving of the *burnous* which she had started. When she had finished it, she brought it to Si Ahmed.

" This *burnous* is well woven," he said, " and thou art a clever worker ; but thou knowest thou art free, Aïcha, and that nothing obliges thee to stay here."

" *Sidi*, thou hast granted me liberty, and yet I still consider myself thy slave. Where else would I go in this city where I know no one? Who else would protect me if I were attacked? Keep me with thee — "

She spoke in a tone she tried to keep calm, but in her words beat the fear of his refusal.

" So be it," he said. " Stay as long as God wills."

Aïcha went back to her work. This time she put on her loom the chain of a carpet, and the chain had so many threads and the patterns the girl invented were so beautiful with blending colors, that the carpet took as long to weave as three great *burnouses*. And as she worked and lived on in Si Ahmed's house which had become her own, he found that she had become as necessary to him as the air he breathed. And yet he dared not ask for her. When she brought in his tea he would have found it too daring to say, "Stay." But fire warmed his blood.

He felt it — he would have the gentle figure of this girl constantly beside him, lean over her eyes, press on hers his trembling lips, draw her to him in an embrace ever closer.

One day, without saying anything, he left for the *Sous* and asked her parents for Aïcha's hand. He paid them a generous *sadecq*. When he returned Aïcha had finished her carpet. It graced their marriage chamber.

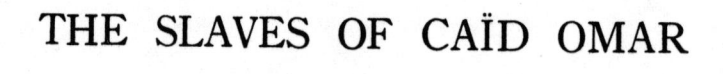

THE SLAVES OF CAÏD OMAR

CHAPTER IX

THE SLAVES OF CAÏD OMAR

Caïd Omar was a rich and powerful man. He reigned over a prosperous tribe and knew and practiced as well as the next the art of " making the *burnous* sweat " — which in no way discredited him in the eyes of his subjects.

Although he might legitimately have taken the four wives that the Prophet allows to the faithful, he had married only one, Khadouj.

She, belonging to a family of notables herself, would tolerate no co-wife, and so Caïd Omar had chosen his concubines from among his slaves. Three of them especially pleased him : Fatma, Johra and Kheïta.

These girls stood in great fear of their master. It is impossible to feel affection for one who imposes himself, but they had to pretend to be devoted to him. To enjoy the master's favor meant a chance of receiving gifts of trinkets, silks and *caftans*.

The *caid* possessed two adjoining houses in the city of Fez. Khadouj was installed in the larger. The three slave concubines lived in the other. Caïd Omar had only to open a door and follow a passageway when he wished to visit his slaves. This situation was quite convenient for him.

His official functions often called him, and for a considerable time, into the *bled*. He never attempted to take Khadouj with him. Being a true native of Fez she could not conceive of life as possible outside her own city and had been careful to stipulate in her marriage contract that under no pretext could her husband make her leave it.

So the *caid* departed with his three slaves, for the Prophet — on whom benediction and peace?! — has said that it is not good for man to live alone.

[99]

The three girls journeyed on mule-back. Their *haiks* of white wool covered them up to the eyes. When the road was deserted they made bold to let them down ; they breathed the pure air and saw the immensity of the *bled* unroll before them. They saw, too, the lines of trees, one following the other, which border the road and thought that the Nazarenes who planted them there must have strange ideas indeed.

When Caïd Omar was among his tribe, all sorts of duties fell to him. He had little time for his slaves then, and they, left unguarded, fell into temptation. They each took a lover and chose him from among the many negroes their master owned.

One night, at home again in Fez, the *caid* called to him the slave named Kheïta. This was contrary to his usual custom. When at Fez he never left his wife's room ; but Kheïta had become necessary to him. Although she was not more beautiful than her companions, she was more loving and the *caid* had bought her only a short time before.

When Fatma and Johra saw Kheïta come out of their master's chamber, they were violently jealous and showed it to the favorite by the thousand and one underhand provocations that spiteful women make use of. One day — oh quite accidentally — Kheïta received boiling water on her foot. Another day she found her prettiest *sebenia* torn, her newest *caftan* soiled.

Complain to the *sidi?* Kheïta would have done so gladly but she dared not for fear of reprisals ; her spite could only pile up in her heart. She thought out a way of avenging herself and bided her time.

One night her two companions took their lovers into their room. After boiling the water, they made tea and all commenced to drink cosily together.

" We have no cakes," said Kheïta casually, " but the *Lella* told me to buy some this morning and I saw that she forgot to lock the chest where they are kept."

This was her pretext to get out without suspicion. She ran to the adjoining dwelling. There the *caid* lay beside his wife. She slipped to the door of their room.

" Master," she called, " Master, get up — "

Caïd Omar waked abruptly and growled,

" What is the matter? "

Instead of answering directly, Kheïta repeated more urgently, "Master, get up, I say. You must. . . ."

It was only when he stood before her that she added, in a whisper, " Lord, those dogs and daughters of dogs, in whom thou believest, have betrayed thee. They are sinning with thy negroes, Youssef and Abd-Salam."

It is not a good thing to be the bearer of ill tidings. The *caid's* anger was so violently aroused that Kheïta bore the first shock of it.

" Daughter of lies! May the sea be over thee! Thou shalt 'eat of the stick' as thou hast never before eaten — "

But truth carries in itself something that convinces and disturbs. Even as the *caid* thundered at Kheïta, " Thou liest," he knew that what she had said was true. He scarcely took the time to throw his *burnous* over his shoulders. Rage shot him from the room.

He crossed the patio and ran through the door that separated the two dwellings. He did not even try to muffle the sound of his *babouches*. As he advanced he thundered at his slaves, " Youssef! Abd-Salam! "

The two men recognized the voice of their lord and ceased their drinking. The women ran to hide in a corner. The bones of all four weakened with terror.

Youssef was the negro nearest the door. He was big and powerful. Sometimes, to gain attention or admiration, he would take pieces of iron in his hands and bend them as easily as a child would a bit of *kessera*.

Seizing one of the massive metal candlesticks on the floor, he awaited the moment when his master would have to stoop to enter the low door such as are built into the portals of native houses ; then he struck him two blows on the head.

Blood spurted with such force that the negro's *gandourah* was splattered. The *caid* cried out once and fell like an ox whose throat has been slit. At the same moment the two negroes took to their heels, the usual behavior of men in such situations. The women were left alone to bear the brunt of it.

Approaching their master the trembling negresses saw that he was not quite dead.

[103]

" Oh misery — " whispered Johra, " when he comes to himself he will punish us beyond belief.   He may take our lives as we would have wished to take his — he will make us suffer forever after — "

A glance at each other meant they should finish the business.   Taking hold of the same candlestick they continued the heavy blows.

However, from the end of the house where she slept, Khadouj had heard her husband cry out.   She threw on a *caftan* and taking the same route the *caid* had, she reached the threshold of the room where he lay lifeless and bleeding.

Kheïta followed her.   They began shouting for help.   " Oh ye faithful, come to save a life!   Come to save a life!"

Their screams were piercing.   One of the *pasha's* policemen who lived in the same street heard them but did not heed them.   Later, to excuse himself, he said, " I only thought the *caid* was correcting one of his wives," and the explanation was so plausible that it was accepted by his chief.

Morning brought the crime to light.   The negroes who had fled the city at the opening of the gates were not caught but the two guilty women were arrested.   Cherifian justice sentenced them to six years in prison. Even if they had not committed the crime they had been accomplices and had finished it off.

When I saw them they were serving their sentence.   By a curious streak of chance the city of Fez, needing a prison for women, had bought the house of Caïd Omar, which his heirs had put on sale as none of them wanted to live in a place where blood had been spilled.   The negresses were thus imprisoned in the house that had been theirs.

I saw them one afternoon, squatting in a ray of sunlight in a corner of the patio.   They worked without haste, making *couffins* from sprigs of *doum*.   An old Arifa sentry watched them.

Except that they were clad in the drab gray prisoner's *caftan* and that they were forbidden to go on the roof, their way of living was not much altered.

Their bedroom was the very one in which the murder had been committed.   On their rush mats they slept there perfectly sound.

They knew that I knew of their crime and seemed to feel no shame before me.   Not even remorse.   Their great dark pupils in the yellowish whites examined me curiously.   When I asked them, " How could you have committed such a crime? " Johra, who is older, answered for herself and her partner, " It was the will of Allah.   Allah desires that there be ' Fatmas ' in prison."

WHAT HAPPENED TO MAHJOUB AND THE RECOMMENDATION THAT HAD BEEN GIVEN HIM

CHAPTER X

WHAT HAPPENED TO MAHJOUB AND THE RECOMMENDATION THAT HAD BEEN GIVEN HIM

A few years ago a Captain Marchand, who was garrisoned at Marrakech, was petitioned by a simple old native called Mahjoub. He was an ex-Moroccan trooper.

Mahjoub was without work. In the time of the old *Maghzen* he could have sold the military outfit in which the *cherifian* government had dressed him and would then have presented himself to his chief who, after several licks of the strap on his back, would have dressed him anew. But only his single *gandourah* and a threadbare *djellaba* remained to him. Besides this, he had a family to look after. The eldest of his daughters, named Fatma, worked for Captain Marchand.

" *Sidi*," she said each morning to her master, when bringing his boots or serving his coffee, " *Sidi*, I have no one except thee to ask a favor of. Thou who art a great man, thou who hast a long arm — long as from here to Koutoubia — thou mightst recommend my father to one of the chiefs, thou mightst find some employment for him."

The captain was careful not to answer, " I am not a great man," for it was necessary to guard his prestige in the eyes of the natives, but he was not unmindful of the obligations of a master toward his servants; he replied,

" Very well, Fatma, I will see — "

The difficulty was that Mahjoub did not know how to do anything except hold a rifle and mount guard. There was no opening for him in the French administration where it was necessary, at the least, to understand the French language. Thinking it over, the captain decided the best thing to do would be to recommend Mahjoub to the *khalifa* of the *pasha*. In a large city like Marrakech the *pasha* has many openings suitable for an ex-trooper.

The captain sent for the fellow. " Would you like to be a sentry at the inner gates of the city? "

" *Inch Allah, sidi.* "

" Would you like to be a *moualindour?* You could guard the quarters during the night and see that nothing happened."

" The benediction of Allah on thee, *sidi.*"

" I am going to give you a note to the *khalifa* of the *pasha;* go to him in my name."

The captain wrote a few words, folded the paper, handed it to Mahjoub. The latter took it, held it slanting the better to see, then, just as he had seen it done at the *fqih*, he examined its lines from right to left. Satisfied apparently, though he had not understood a word, he undertook putting the letter away. A native has no pocket, but he has his *djellaba*. Its hood is an excellent and safe place to hide treasures.

Everybody in Marrakech knows the *pasha's* house. Not far from the mosque of Bab-Doukkala, its great length takes up almost the entire side of a long, dusty street. High doorways with beautiful projections of carved cedar draw the passer's attention. Lined up like onions on either side of these folding doors, innumerable natives squat continually on their heels, waiting for days and weeks, sometimes, for the moment of an audience.

Naturally these petitioners are never received by the *pasha* himself. His Excellency El Hadj el Glaoui has other fish to fry. But they consider themselves happy, they thank Allah the All-merciful when, after an honorable *fabor* — the *fabor* is a national institution in a *cherifian* country — they are permitted to state their case to a servant of the lowest servant of the lowest secretary of his Excellency the *pasha*.

Mahjoub took his place in line. He was not bored. There is nothing livelier than the street of the *pasha's* dwelling. It leads to the *souks* and offers a continual and varied spectacle ; laden camels with a sleepwalker's step, donkeys hard-driven by their masters, women heavily bundled in *haiks*, lean little girls with deep-set eyes, carrying piles of round *kesseras* balanced on planks to the baking house. Beasts and men, they all push, jostle, elbow each other in the sunlight, the noise and the dust.

After two days of waiting, Mahjoub succeeded in getting the letter he bore accepted by one of the *Mokhraznis* who passed it to another *Mokhrazni* who confided it to a *chaouch* who passed it to a secretary who in turn communicated it to its destination — the *khalifa* of the *pasha*.

The latter at first threw a distrait glance at the request, then, seeing that it came from a European with whom he had often dealt, he stopped what he was doing to call a *Mokhrazni*.

" The native who brought in this letter — don't let him get away," he said. " I'll take up his case in a moment."

Mahjoub was waiting outside in the street. The *Mokhrazni* went out to find him. Beside him the old fellow crossed the wide entrance-court where, in the *benikas* opening on the galleries, scribes sat writing on their knees exactly in the position that the Prophet Mohamed must have assumed — and it cannot have been a comfortable one — when he wrote the first *surah* of the Koran on a sheep's shoulder bone.

The *Mokhrazni* led Mahjoub to a corner of one of the patios. " Stay right here. The *khalifa* will see thee when he is free."

At noon the great administrative machine which is the dwelling of the *pasha* ceases to function. The *khalifa*, who had completely forgotten old Mahjoub, left for dinner. The *Mokhrazni* did likewise. However, before leaving he called to one of his comrades on guard, and pointing to Mahjoub commanded, " The *khalifa* said he must see this chap when he has time."

It so happened on that afternoon that the *pasha* sent his *khalifa* into the *bled* on a matter of business. The *khalifa* did not return to his office. Toward three o'clock the *Mokhrazni* who watched over Mahjoub also went off. Mindful of his duty, he passed the word to the man replacing him. Old Mahjoub was still squatting in his corner.

" That fellow over there," said the *Mokhrazni*, pointing, " see that he doesn't move from here. The *khalifa* wants to see him."

The end of the afternoon came. Mahjoub who began to be hungry thought of going home. He had not taken two steps in that direction before the *Mokhrazni* who was detailed to watch him clutched him by the shoulder.

"Where goest thou, dog?"

"Home," replied the honest Mahjoub.

"Allah! Allah! Thou art trying to escape," cried the *Mokhrazni*, who was an excellent *Mokhrazni*. "Thou wouldst like to see me in prison in thy place!"

And to show Mahjoub at once the sort of a *Mokhrazni* he was, he commenced to administer to the old codger a magisterial blow with his fist on the nose.

Mahjoub, well, old Mahjoub was an ex-trooper. . . . Up to now his rôle had been to deal blows and avoid getting them. He lammed back. The *Mokhrazni* called for help. His comrades came running. They were many. Well-aimed blows fell from all sides on the old chap's head.

In vain he tried to explain that he was not a criminal; every time he opened his mouth he took a fresh blow and some one yelled at him, "Shut up!"

Things were at this stage when Boua-sidi appeared on the scene. Boua-sidi is very much of a personage in Marrakech; he is the chief of native police. He had arrived on the way from the mosque where he had just been saying his prayers. When he saw his men armed with whips and all hot from battle, when he perceived Mahjoub sunk on the ground with blood all over his face, he demanded official explanation. His men gave it to him superabundantly.

"*Sidi*, this goof here was trying to escape. The khalifa did not have time to see him before he left for the *bled* but he left orders to watch him closely."

The chief of police let fall a contemptuous glance on Mahjoub.

"Dog! You've got a nerve! Trying to escape! Well, I'll teach you —"

And turning to his men, speaking with the precision, the brusque authority that marks the chief,

"Bind this man and take him to jail."

The *Mokhraznis*, cudgels in hand led off poor Mahjoub.

At this time the *pasha's* jails were installed in the subterranean vaults

which stretch beneath the palace of a sultan whose fabulous riches gained him the name of " the Golden."

Of that marvelous palace, of which the gazelle was jealous, say the Arab poets, little remains except a few tiles half covered over at one of the roof tops ; but the vaults were so solidly built that neither time nor men, still more destructive, could destroy them.

Nothing could be worse than these vaults transformed into prisons.

You cross a dusty esplanade where once flourished an emperor's gardens, you go down some fifteen steps. Whoever has been designated as your guide carries an acetylene lamp. You reach the catacombs in pitch darkness ; not even a ray of light can penetrate that far.

In the lamp's glaring flare, you can just distinguish the vast passages that lead into each other ; sometimes there is a door opening in the walls, more often it is merely a hole, just wide enough to let a man through. The prisoners are led in through this. There is not the least danger of their being able to escape. In the altogether improbable case, however, that they might reach the entrance, they would have found it barred by a chain and guarded.

Imagine a European jailed in that. At the end of twenty-four hours he would be dead, and more from mental than from physical suffering. Some way, the native survives it. The belief in fatalism can lead to the absurd, undoubtedly, but it engenders patience and resignation.

Four or five days went by. Mahjoub's wife was not disturbed when her husband did not return ; it sometimes happened that he left Marrakech on chance employment without being able to notify his family.

On his part, Captain Marchand thought that the old man had obtained the place asked for him.

As for Mahjoub himself, the honest and unfortunate Mahjoub who was mouldering in his jail without *kessera*, without water, he had leisure to imagine himself back in the time of the ancient *Maghzen* when the exchequer was empty — for the distribution of victuals to the *mehallas* was subject to a whimsical irregularity.

However, he was right not to despair. Captain Marchand did chance to meet up with the *khalifa* of the *pasha*.

" You found work for old Mahjoub," he said, " and I thank you."

" Mahjoub? Who is he? That person you sent to me? By the way, what became of him? "

" What do you mean, what became of him? "

" I told him to wait so I could speak to him. I didn't get back — "

Up to now things had happened promptly, simply, and on the whole, logically. Now they became complicated and halted in their step.

The captain ordered an investigation to be made. The investigation ended, the *khalifa* ordered the prisoner released. But, if it is easy for a man to get into prison, it is not the same about getting out. In cherifian jails there is a *fqih*, a *fqih* with all its red tape to disentangle. At the entrance of the vaults turned into prisons there is a sentry.

Good Moroccans as they were, the *fqih* and the sentry could only act by means of a *fabor*. Impossible to give it to them directly. It was necessary to pass through a series of intermediary *Mokhraznis* and the *chaouch* who are also good Moroccans and have need of *flouss* to live. A week was required to affect Mahjoub's release.

One morning Captain Marchand saw him entering his office. The frightful sojourn in prison had not blighted the old fellow; his good sense had remained sound.

" What was written on the paper that thou gavest me? " he demanded of Captain Marchand. " It was that paper that threw me in prison."

" Good Lord, Mahjoub, there has been a mistake — it was not my fault. It will never happen again. I am going to give you another letter. You go —"

Mahjoub bore no grudge, but his mistrust for whatever was written on paper was rife.

" Ah," he murmured, " I thank thee, I want no more letters of introduction. If thou desirest to procure me a place thyself, all right. — Otherwise, praise Allah, I will hunt work for myself."

IN THE HOME OF SI ABDERRAHAMEN

CHAPTER XI

IN THE HOME OF SI ABDERRAHAMEN

I had not seen Marrakech for three years when I returned this time. In the vicinity of Demaa el F'na and Koutoubia the native quarters were much changed. There had been all sorts of " modern improvements " in the way of new construction. Just as in certain Parisian streets, European shops and cafés had opened up under the crumbling old arcades. But elsewhere, praise be to Allah, everything looked the same as of old.

The *souks* offered their everlasting teeming native life — a labyrinth resounding with the cries of " *Balek, balek* " (gangway!), with dust rising from the dried mud ground to a roofing of interlaced reeds.

Everything in the narrow way hustles and jostles ; donkeys, resigned victims; heavy camels with pompous profiles ; flying little girls with grasshopper bodies swathed in colorful rags ; charming young boys whose shining eyes have not yet learned to conceal their thoughts ; women hampered by their ochre *haiks*, who, beneath the pink or blue or lilac *litham*, seemed garbed in carnival costumes ; heavier masculine *burnouses* or *djellabas* that loiter or hurry about their affairs. . . .

" I shall come to meet thee," Si Abderrahamen had told me when I announced my desire to visit them, " for thou wouldst never find my house alone."

He appears at the corner of an alley off the street of the *souks*, a wide bourgeois face that might have been modeled out of lard and adorned with a beard hewn of jet. He extends a ceremonious hand, bows his head wrapped in its winter cowl, broadly smiles.

" Greeting, madame. All is well with thee? (Or " No harm with thee? ")

" Greeting, Si Abderrahamen. All is well. How is the ' home '? "

" The ' home ' is well. She awaits thy coming."

[119]

Side by side we move on in the crowd. The narrow, overhanging streets multiply their windings and turnings. We pass under ancient gates whose horse-shoe-shaped archways open into sombre vaulted passages. We are in the Kessaria.

Here beats the commercial heart of Marrakech, capital of South Morocco.

Dark, mysterious, the *fondouks* crowd upon each other. The oldest of them are decorated with fine copper-studded portals ; friezes in plaster display their marvelously fragile reliefs ; under the balconies formed by the second story, balustraded with openwork carving, bales of Roubaix cloth, Rouen and Manchester cottons and sumptuous silks from Lyons are piled.

Squatting in the patios shoulder to shoulder, *burnouses* of soft gray-pearl or sombre Carmelite brown discuss the exchange rates in whispers — a monotonous murmur rising in the air like prayers to *flouss* the god of the place.

My companion halts at the far end of a blind alley. A moment before autos had honked in my ears, I had met my own countrymen ; although I knew myself to be in far-off South Morocco, I had felt the immediate contact with our Western civilization. But Si Abderrahamen pushes open a portal before me, I cross a threshold, I pass through a darkened, twisted passage, and suddenly I am transported into long-gone ages.

Si Abderrahamen's house has not the dimensions of a palace but it is enchanting.

Mosaics are everywhere. Their thousand tiny squares cover the floor, brighten the walls, decorate the columns, and climb to the second story. They are so exactly adjusted that the jointure is invisible and they give one the sensation of being enclosed in some hard, brilliant, unbreakable material whose warm blue hue is picked out in arabesques of topaz. All this fairylike background creates an unreal, a precious atmosphere adapted to the mysterious voluptuousness which we insist on according to the Orient.

In the center of the house the patio bears the stamp of a long-forgotten architect's perfect taste. In the nearest room, on one of the mattresses that range the walls, Lella Zohra awaits me.

I know beyond a doubt that beauty is a relative thing and one's appreciation personal, but I believe that the few Westerners who have caught sight of Si Abderrahamen's present wife will agree about her — negroid features, pop-eyes, she is ugly. When she gives an amiable smile she is uglier still, her thick lips drawing back over toothless gums blackened by pomegranate peel.

Immediately cordial, however, she makes me welcome. At the same time as she, a visitor who has preceded me arises, a Frenchwoman, Mlle. M. We all take our places against the wall.

Seated at the right of the door, Lella Zohra prepares the tea. The harmony of her ample garments, their clear contrasting colors, make a joyous rhythm that lights up the whole long room.

The measured movements take on something of the air of a ritual — a pinch of green tea, big handfuls of mint, boiling water which must be poured slowly, slabs of sugar which must melt, manifold and devotional tastings to judge when the concoction is just right.

Mlle. M., just back from an excursion into the Atlas, tells how she managed to join a caravan of prospectors, rough but loyal companions, with whom she traveled several days.

" Strangers," she remarks, " are coming to Morocco more and more each year." Then addressing Si Abderrahamen directly, " Probably this does not please you? "

Her question comes as a surprise to her host. His black eyes open wide and roll toward her.

Mlle. M. insists on an answer. With people brought up to roundabout ways, it is sometimes best to come straight to the point. " Si Abderrahamen, what is thought in Morocco of French rule? "

The eyes of the Marrakechi roll anew in their sockets ; he makes a face as though a bone were lodged in his throat and refused to budge.

" *Ia*, madame, how wouldst thou have me answer? "

I can think of nothing better than this as a way of getting out of answering and I tell him so. Then slowly — not to hunt a word, for he speaks excellent French, but to give himself a chance to weigh their import — Si Abderrahamen begins,

" There is one thing that we all appreciate since you came."

" What is that? "

As if a sudden uneasiness assailed him, he hesitates. " Thou wilt not repeat what I am going to say, thou wilt not make trouble for me? "

" Certainly not."

" Well, if thou couldst, in the *souks*, speak with the people, especially with humble people, thou wouldst gather from all lips the same statement. Since the French occupation we feel safer. Before that no one would have dared leave his house after ten o'clock ; at present we know we have nothing to be afraid of. Our wives and daughters can go about their business without fear of being kidnapped."

" Hem, as for that, Si Abderrahamen —"

" Yes I know to what ye allude. Last year three maidens were carried off, but remember that their abductors were so swiftly pursued and overtaken that the girls were returned to their families before anything irreparable had occurred. Before that the kidnappers had time to get the girl to a great distance. When, after weeks and months, her people by the best of luck succeeded in finding a trace of their child, it was but to learn that she had been sold. Concubine of her master, she was perhaps already a mother.

" Before this, just around Marrakech, I can say without exaggerating that two thousand little girls were sold yearly. It was a profitable trade. A pretty child never changed hands for less than four thousand francs. From mouth to ear only there was whispered the name of an inhabitant of this town — a great personage even — who fattened on this sort of trade.

" His agents chose very young children. Afterward, in his palace, they were decked out, painted and appareled. When they knew how to sing and dance and please in every way, they were detailed into lots of four and sold for sixty or eighty thousand francs to some rich Moroccan desiring to stock his harem."

" Is it possible? "

" Such things are well known. The kidnappers worked — and even still work, for the Protectorate government has only a small detachment of police and cannot keep an eye on everything — the kidnappers operated chiefly in the *bled*, in the region of the Sous. Very rarely did they dare

[122]

an abduction in town. They attempted this only if the girl's beauty was remarkable. Their ruse to catch her was simple —

"'If thou wilt carry this parcel to my house there will be a *fabor* in it for thee.'

"The child would follow the man. The house would be that of an accomplice. When the door was opened the child was snared. These stolen children are always those of *meskines*.

"Not all," corrects Mlle. M. "Remember Khadidja — her parents were well-off. One evening two years ago when her father was out and her mother ill, there came a knock at the door. The little thing went to open it. How old was she? — Not more than four. Before she could cry out a hand had seized her shoulder and bore her off. The parents were in despair. The father filed a complaint with the French authorities. They called the police. The town-crier hurried through the streets and *souks*, giving a description of Khadidja. One evening the father as he came home found in his doorway a large bundle from which regular breathing issued. It was his child whom someone had brought back asleep."

While we were talking, Lella Zohra had finished the tea. She half filled the tiny glasses traced in gold on the copper tray.

Mina, the eldest daughter, takes each one and offers them to us in turn. She comes and goes across the room with movements of natural grace. Her *caftan* made of a heavy red and yellow brocade falls in unbroken lines, its bright colors softened by the net of the *ferragiat*.

I say to her, "How pretty you are, Mina. What a *caftan*!"

She had been waiting for my compliment; she smiles shyly, "I put it on purposely for thee. It is my favorite."

We drink our tea in small loud sips. Good breeding requires this. It is a way of saying to your hosts, "Thy tea is excellent, I am enjoying it."

Seated facing the door, Si Abderrahamen wears a peaceful mien. — What is he thinking about?

As though he divined my thought, "We were talking about kidnapping," he says. "I was telling thee how easily it occurred in former times. If it would interest thee, would ye like for my wife to tell her story? She has been stolen and sold."

[123]

In the same breath Mlle. M. and I cry out, " You, Lella! "
Zohra smiles bashfully and turns toward her husband instead of answering.

" Thou art asked to relate what happened to thee," he tells her. " Tell it. Thou hast not forgotten it? "

" *Ia, sidi!* By Allah I remember perfectly."

" Tell it then."

Zohra lowers her head and smiles anew. She is " ashamed." Finally she decides to please us.

" One winter evening I was playing under the stars before our house with my sister. We lived in the *bled*."

" How old were you, Lella? "

" Seven or eight years old."

" And your sister? "

" Not more than ten. A neighbor, Aïcha, came over to us one evening. ' I have no more *semoula* for my supper,' she said to us. ' Can mother lend me some? '

" We went inside our house. My mother was in the patio busy washing some beef. She gave us the *semoula*. Aïcha waited outside on the doorstep. ' Come,' she said, ' come with me and I will give thee some candy.'

" As we ran to her she turned the corner of the house. Not wanting to call or waken suspicion, she simply lifted one arm. It was a signal. Two men ran out from behind a heap of offal. Oh my fathers, what faces they had! What turbans, what *djellabas!* All over holes. . . ."

" ' Here they are,' Aïcha said, pointing to us.

" The men threw themselves on us. We tried to cry out, but they held their hands over our mouths.

" ' Be still!' they said. ' If you are not still we will eat you up.' Not far off were their donkeys. They dropped each of us in a *chouari* (double basket), covered us with a cloth and green branches and started on their way. The sky was clear ; the night cold ; the beasts trotted fast — the men were in a hurry to get there. From time to time I tried to lift the cloth, to peek my head between the branches, but each time I did I got a blow from a stick and heard a voice say, ' Hide thyself!' I

cried and cried. Then to hush me up one of the men offered me some dates.

"We traveled all night. The cries of *chacals* sounded in the *bled* and the howls of dogs in the villages we passed through. Dawn found us before the rampart of Rabat. The men halted; they hesitated about attempting the gates; they were afraid of getting into trouble if anyone lifted the cloth or the branches that covered the *chouari*. But luck was with them. Nobody suspected anything and they were allowed to enter."

At the time of which Lella Zohra speaks, and which is not so distant since it happened about fifteen years ago, the slave market was held at Rabat every afternoon in one of the *fondouks*. The slaves were displayed in little cells built around three sides of the inside court.

"There were few men," explains Lella Zohra. "Women are preferred as slaves. They give more service. The public crier led those who were up for auction around the courtyard. He called out the offers,

"'Oh believers! Here is a buyer for twenty-five, for thirty, for thirty-five *douros* — thirty-five *douros*, that's not dear!'"

Si Abderrahamen who had finished his tea sets down his glass and interrupts his wife.

"The French have done well to suppress those slave markets. To lead those women around like beasts — Moslem though I am I could not endure to see it. It was worse when they were old women — no one wanted them. They were mocked at as they passed, attention called to their signs of age. The dealer could only succeed in getting rid of them by putting them in lots with the young ones."

In the charming setting about us the picture called up by Si Abderrahamen seems the more revolting. There is a moment's silence. Mlle. M. breaks it.

"Poor Lella Zohra. You have been sold in a market!"

"*Ia*, madame, what sayest thou! My sister, yes, — not I. The one who had stolen me led me to one of the houses in the city. A rich merchant who had heard me spoken of happened to be there. I was ordered to fetch him a glass of tea. He watched me.

"'My right hand acquires her (buys her),' he said. 'I will make a gift of her to the "home."'"

[127]

" The price was discussed and quickly accepted.   The one who was to be my master paid over eighty *douros*.   I was worth more, but it is unwise to haggle over stolen goods."

" Did you ever see your parents again? "

" Never again."

" And your neighbor, Aïcha? "

" Aïcha!   That dog of Satan! — Don't speak her name.   If I saw her again I would strangle her myself."

Speaking according to our lights, Mlle. M. exclaims, " How unhappy you must have been with your masters! "

" Oh, my fathers, on the contrary, I was happy.   Without a doubt I ' Eat of the stick ' more than once, but I deserved it."

" Slaves are not mishandled in Morocco," confirms Si Abderrahamen. " When it turns out that they are ill-nourished, badly clothed or over-worked, they have the right to demand to be sold."

" But what if the master doesn't want to do that? "

Zohra hides a smile behind her hand.   " There is always a way to make him."

" How? "

She giggles anew.   To her my question is extremely simple-minded. " *Ia*, madame, it is so easy. — You break everything from clumsiness. You do naught that is bidden you or else you do it all wrong.   One day the master will yell out, ' Get out, you daughter of sin!   Off with you! I've had enough of this.   The next one that buys you will have no thanks for Allah.' . . ."

" But what if the master is stubborn, if he wants to show his slave that he is stronger than she is? "

" There is left the means of escape.   It is easy over the roof tops."

" That happened no later than yesterday," comes from Mlle. M. " Four slaves fled from the house of Gonndafil and took refuge in the ' Services Municipaux.'   ' Look,' they said to one of the adjutants, ' are our clothes befitting a slave of a noble of the *Maghzen?*   Look at our hollow cheeks. . . .' — To tell the truth, they did not appear ill-clothed or under-nourished."

Lella Zohra's shoulders shrug.   " Those women acted unwisely.

Supposing they had been hungry with their master — they will be hungrier still now that they are free. How can they obtain *flouss?*"

"They will work."

"Work at what? They know no trade. Moslem women are not taught any. They will be loitering in the streets; next they will become 'daughters of joy.'"

For the third time as prescribed by the *caïda*, Mina takes around the glasses of tea. She stoops, raises again. Under the glare of light that reflects the brilliant surface of tile from every side, the silken stuff of her *caftan* shimmers in sudden contrasts. The tea's perfume fills every corner.

"Finish your story for us, Lella Zohra," begs Mlle. M.

Zohra's eyebrows lift and her hand outlines a gesture. "It is not interesting to ladies like thee."

"Come, tell us."

Zohra resumes in her hoarse voice that lends an air of savagery to her least words.

"My master's wife had children that were still small. At first she treated me as one of them. I shared their games and was fed in the same way. I learned to crush grain, to weave and embroider along with the daughters of the house; they let me attend the classes in the Koran which a *tholba* came to hold. I know by heart all the *surahs* that it is lawful for a woman to know. Later on the other slaves taught me the household duties; the slave who cooked taught me that."

Zohra ceases and looks toward us, smiling. There, she seems to say, that is about all.

Above the patio the yellow crescent moon proclaims the fall of night. With a quick movement Zohra presses the switch. Light floods the lamp. The blue of the tiles scintillates with renewed vigor. She gets up. Preparations for supper require her presence in the little dark cell that serves as kitchen. Mina busies herself gathering together the glasses scattered about the chamber; then she, too, leaves us. We see nothing more of her except her *caftan* in fleeting instants gliding like a flame past the open door.

The last-born of the house plays quietly among the arcades. Not a sound. There is an inexpressible feeling of peace.

[129]

Sitting on folded legs among the cushions, Si Abderrahamen's face is beatific in its immobility. One of us remarks, " *Sidi*, you are a very happy man."

He makes no movement, gives no start, but a mask drops over his face. Each time a question is put to him he assumes an air of mystery, as if one had asked him to betray a state secret — his head might be at stake. He never makes an immediate response. Evidently he asks himself, " Now, will this compromise me? "

" Then you are not happy? " insists Mlle. M.

" I am perfectly happy, madame. All I need to do is to let myself live. My wife is busy, energetic, intelligent. No household could be better kept, better ornamented with cushions, rugs, embroideries ; in none could you eat better cooking. Besides, my wife is a woman of good counsel. If a time comes when I don't know what to do, I ask her advice."

" And never follow it! "

" Don't deceive thyself, madame. I take it when it is good."

" Then your wife leads you," teases Mlle. M.

" Allah! Allah! She leads me? " — But, after all, that is the case of most Moroccan husbands. Why is the legend of Moslem wives trembling before their masters spread among ye? Those of ye who come into our harems know that is not so."

I laugh. " So the Moroccan women are cleverer than Western ones ; they know better how to manage you. How do they do it? "

" They are not more clever," retorts Si Abderrahamen. " They are not more intelligent, in fact. If they lead their husbands there are special reasons for it, reasons that do not exist elsewhere."

" Indeed? Tell us what they are."

Si Abderrahamen is silent. Again he is choked with reticence. It is ever the way with Moroccans. You think you have lifted one corner of the veil that covers their private life ; the veil falls again.

But I insist. " Is it something one may not know? "

Si Abderrahamen speaks in lowered, prudent tones, " *Ia*, madame, what if Zohra should hear me. . . ."

" She is busy in the kitchen."

" How shall I answer what ye ask? — The minds of our women are full of superstition, — magic rites which religion condemns but which are still used. To obtain what they desire, to guard themselves from what they fear, they turn to sorcery. With us, husbands are always afraid that their wives may feed them some fatal concoction without their knowing it. Usually they take this precaution : ' On condition that thou usest no magic art, that thou addest no powders to my food,' they tell their wives, ' I leave thee free to do exactly as thou wilt in the house. Order, take charge of everything.' "

The tea and rice cakes have beguiled my hunger and without noticing it I have let my usual dinner hour slip by. When I get up it is late.

Polite and courteous host that he is, Si Abderrahamen insists on accompanying me home. A faintly pink, almost immaterial moon floats against the divinely pure night sky. In the *souks* there is a greater bustle than by day. *Burnouses* and *haiks* form a single grayish surge under the garish flare of acetylene lights. Every other moment we press against the merchants' booths to let a donkey or herb-laden camel pass by. In the air floats the penetrating odor of hot bread and fresh mint.

As we walk along I express to Si Abderrahamen my surprise at hearing his daughter answer me in French. " Where did she learn it? "

" In school with the French nuns."

" Does she seem clever? "

" They think she is very clever. The sisters wanted to push her to pass her examinations, but I was not pleased at that."

" Why not? "

Again the too direct question disconcerts Si Abderrahamen. He is torn between the desire to hold his peace and the fear of offending me if he does not answer.

" *Ia*, madame, our customs are irreconcilable. Mina is going on twelve. She begins to show signs of independence. When her European playmates were taken to the moving pictures she wanted to go with them, crying, ' *Sidi, Baba*, the others are allowed to go.' I answered, ' It is not the same thing for you, ' but she wept and sulked. I should have used the switch, but it is not the custom now — now no one dares whip his own children. I thought to myself,

" Take heed! Mina weeps now to go to the moving pictures, which

[131]

is nothing. But leave her two years more in the French school and then tell her, ' Thou art to marry such and such a man — it is settled between his father and myself,' and she will answer, ' I am sorry, *Sidi*, *Baba*, but I will choose my own husband.'

" The result? — My daughter will be left on my hands with all her learning. I have taken the pretext that she is of an age to be veiled to remove her from school and close her up in the house. She wept at first, but she has become used to it. Now if someone proposed to take her out, she would refuse."

We had neared my hotel. Crouching against the wall a beggar lifts up her moving plaint, " Oh ye that can rejoice the heart by a few francs — "

Through the roofing of reeds above the street each star is a marvelous golden nail-point ; far above the human uproar mounts the loud cry of the *souks*, " *Balek*, *balek*. . . ."

My companion halts. He extends his hand, " Go with peace."

" Stay with the good."

For the last time Si Abderrahamen bows his head and from his lips falls upon me the native formula of thanks,

" The blessing of Allah upon thee. . . ."

"THOU HAST ONLY TO DROP THIS POWDER
INTO THE WATER HE DRINKS"

CHAPTER XII

" THOU HAST ONLY TO DROP THIS POWDER INTO THE WATER HE DRINKS "

When a sudden death occurs in one of the native homes, the members of the family and friends are struck with a sort of pale terror, and as it is natural for human beings to seek explanations for events, they whisper to one another, " There has been a poisoning. . . ."

That poisonings take place in the harems is an all too certain fact. We can be sure of one thing, however — they are far fewer than the natives say and far more frequent than we know about.

Moroccan households have no contact with the outside world, and this is a very convenient thing for hushing up secrets. The women of the *Moghreb* boast openly among themselves of possessing fatal prescriptions. The venom of vipers, the essence of toxic weeds — they say they understand how to dose them so precisely, so subtly, that they can at will cause death to a victim in the same hour or after lingering weeks. Then death seems to be the outcome of illness.

Do the inmates of the *ayal* really possess this dread power? It is doubtful. " Their knowledge is both uncertain and obscure," say the French who have lived in Morocco for years. " They deceive themselves as to the cause of suspicious deaths. Where there is only a coincidence, they pretend to see a consequence."

But let us not be too sure. There are certainly some dangerous formulas in existence in the various harems. They are handed down in families, as is fitting for such useful things. Mothers transmit them to their daughters. They may serve — one never knows!

When Lella Hadra became a widow and returned to live with her parents, her eighteen years made her appear still a maiden. Allah had

[135]

not given her a child — he alone is all-powerful — and for her husband's death she felt only the feeblest regret.

Thinking of her future, she conceived the idea of marrying her cousin Ali. She had played with him when she was a tiny girl. He was handsome, well-mannered, singularly pleasing, and in the depths of her heart she was in love with him.

Moslem law allows a widow to remarry according to her choice, but there is a vast void between what one may do and what one really does do.

The obligatory four months of seclusion for widows had barely elapsed when Hadra's father said to her,

" Si-Kaddour-ben-Ibrahim wishes to marry thee. He is one of my friends. I have answered with an acceptance."

Like a dutiful daughter, Hadra bowed her young head. She had never even seen the man to whom she was pledged.

" Since Si-Kaddour-ben-Ibrahim pleases thee, *sidi*, he pleases me," she answered. " Since thou lovest him, I will love him. . . ."

Some time afterward, as the young woman was on her way to the baths, she met, in the narrow street, one of the city notables mounted on his mule. Two negroes escorted him. The mule's high saddle was covered with a scarlet cloth. Lella Hadra ventured a glance at him who sat in it. His *burnous*, looped up on the animal's croup, displayed a white woolen sock sustained by green garters — the Prophet's color — above the sock the leg hung, flabby and hairy.

Lella Hadra looked on upward to the old man's face and barely restrained a cry. Was it not Satan himself sprung up before her? The great wine-red nostrils were inflamed and consumed by a hideous disease ; around the gangrened mouth a Nazarene dentist had applied a set of shining false teeth. — Above them, puffy and strangely reddish lips gave the old man a fearsome aspect.

Lella Hadra and her women pushed back against the wall. Rider and slaves passed by in the dust. For another moment the ample *haik* of the gentleman and the yellow *gandourahs* of his escort were visible, then shadow absorbed them.

" Who was he? " Lella Hadra demanded of the eldest of her women.

" The very one that thy father has pledged thee to marry : Si-Kaddour-ben-Ibrahim."

" Allah! Allah ! " cried Hadra.   " He is old enough to be my grandfather — his face is terrifying ! "

" The face of a rich man is never ugly," replied old Fatma sedately. " It were easier to count the grains of sand in the desert than the *douros* contained in Si-Kaddour's coffers."

The contract was already signed.   It was impossible to break it.   The marriage feasts were held.

Hadra passed her " seven fig days " in bitter tears.   However, her spouse at least was generous.   He had bought a sewing machine for her, a phonograph, a wardrobe with a looking-glass door, and a large mirror with a golden frame that had been placed on one of the mattresses against the wall.

Si-Kaddour naïvely believed that his young bride could desire nothing further ; but in the looking glass Hadra studied her pretty round face whose fresh cheeks had made her mother ask, " Hast thou stolen the roses from the sultan's garden? " — Was it for old Kaddour that Allah had given her this flower-face? — She shivered and felt herself falling into the gulf of shades.

Her one comfort was to repeat to herself, " Si-Kaddour is old, very old ; he is sick ; soon Allah will set me free — he alone is merciful."   And, because Si-Kaddour had made a settlement in her favor, she added in her inmost heart, " Then I will marry Ali.   We will have much *flouss* — we will be perfectly happy together."

Contrary to expectation, the old man was stubborn about dying.   A strange thing. — It seemed that Hadra's youth and vigor had passed into his veins and given him new health.

Lella Hadra knew no joy except at the rare intervals when, in her husband's absence, with her old slave as accomplice, she was able to receive visits from her cousin Ali.

What was it they said to one another?   In the chamber of painted beams they were " as the serpent that prepares to strike without warning." One day, taking advantage of the fact of a moment's isolation with his cousin, Ali produced from his *djellaba* a thin package wrapped in paper.

"Here," he said, "is what I promised thee."

Half-opening the paper, Hadra saw a whitish powder within.

"Thou hast only to drop this powder into the water that he drinks," whispered Ali. And when Hadra seemed to hesitate, the young man added,

"There is no other way. Besides, considering the few years that remain to him anyway, we are not robbing him of much."

Two negresses crossed the patio, fetching the water and the samovar for tea. Hadra hid the packet in her *caftan* so dexterously that the slaves never noticed her movement.

Evening came on. Si-Kaddour went to his rest in one of those great brass beds surmounted by a gilded crown which the British manufactured once in series for the notables of Morocco. Sleep overcame him. Lying beside him, young Hadra could not close her eyes. With drumming heart, she awaited the moment when, just before dawn, her husband would arise for his first prayer.

The moment came. The young woman heard Si-Kaddour make his ablutions, recite the sacred words ; then, by the light of the electric globe that illuminated the room, she saw him drink a long draught of water, as was his morning custom. When he finished drinking he made a wry face.

"This water is as briny as the sea," he said. "From what fountain was it drawn?"

From beneath her covers and in a most natural tone, Hadra answered,

"I don't know what thou art talking of. The bad taste is in thy mouth. It happens on waking."

Slowly, gruntingly, the old man got back in bed. The lamp was snapped off now, but through the trellised windows and between the chinks of the door day sent its early rays. Hadra bent over her husband. His head on a woolen cushion, he was sleeping soundlessly, his mouth, as usual, half open.

At first the young woman felt a great relief ; then, immediately, she thought, "In throwing in the powder I forgot to say, 'In the name of Allah.' I must do it over again."

Slaves were coming and going by this time in the patio. Lella Hadra arose to give the orders. The hour having come, she said her prayer and made her toilet.   In the great gilded brass bed Si-Kaddour continued his sleep.

All at once Hadra heard a grunt that sounded like a call.   It came from the far end of the room.   She ran toward it.   Vainly the old man attempted to form some words ; his tongue was paralyzed.   Vainly he tried to move ; it was as if his arms and legs were bound.   Two days later his strength was exhausted.   The Master delivered him from his misery.

The undertaker came to the house to proceed with the greater and lesser ablutions ; the corpse was wrapped in his winding-sheet, a few friends and believers, desirous of acquiring merit in the future life, bore him to the cemetery on a stretcher.   Through the narrow slanting streets of the city, between walls blind and white, the funeral cortege wound its way. In the rear of the dead sounded long-drawn-out pious chanting, " There is no God but God and Mohammed is his Prophet. . . .''

During all this time, secluded in her chamber, Lella Hadra sat bathed in tears ; and, refusing all nourishment, all drink, even as the *caïda* enjoins, seemed to desire but one thing — to die and rejoin her husband.

Two weeks later, when she began to go about again, each Friday she visited the cemetery.   Old Fatma accompanied her.   At the entrance of *Bab-Fetouh* they saluted the dead,

" May Allah grant thee his mercy, to thee even as to my parents and to my ancestors. . . .''

They climbed up among the tombs.   Although that of Si-Kaddour resembled that of so many others — a simple nameless column at the head, Lella Hadra recognized it immediately.

Bowed to the earth she seemed to hold long converse with Si-Kaddour, her late lamented husband.

.   .   .   .

Not long after this the young woman adorned herself in a magnificent yellow *caftan*, arranged all her jewels on head, ears and arms, perfumed herself, painted her hands and feet with henna as for a festival.

Ali, for whom she had sent, came to see her.   He drank the tea which she offered him without seeming to notice that she had beautified herself for his benefit.   When he left her he bore away beneath his *djellaba*, in a pocket of his vest, the two thousand *rei* which represented the price of his services.

Several days passed. One morning, returning from the *souks*, old Fatma remarked to her mistress, " I hear Si-Ali is going to be married. He has paid the *sadecq*."

" How much? " whispered Lella Hadra palely.

" Two thousand *rei*."

The young woman realized now that her money had only served to buy Ali a wife and in her heart she reviled the young man to his farthest relation and called down unthinkable calamities upon his head. At the same time never had she felt so passionate a desire to enjoy her own youth before it fled ; to love and be loved.

As for Ali, once the two thousand *rei* were spent, they seemed to him to be a very small sum for the great service he had rendered.

" One day among days " he went to his cousin. She sat working listlessly at those embroideries in which the *Fascia* excel. Seated on her heels before a loom she was forming with her needle, on a fabric finer than the finest wool, a regular design where arabesques unrolled around rosettes and six-pointed stars.

In a roundabout way he alluded to the demise of Si-Kaddour, to the difficulties he had undergone to procure the poison, of the risks he ran, and ended by claiming a new sum equal to the first.

Lella Hadra listened in silence. She had a clever head. She thought darkly to herself, " If I give in to him to-day, I shall have to give in to-morrow and to-morrow again. There will be no end."

She drew herself up proudly ; she looked toward her cousin in contempt and answered him with a single word,

" Nothing."

Ali's glance, as he left her, went through her like the edge of a sword.

On that same day, at the Moorish café, while sipping a glass of mint-flavored tea with one of his friends, the young man turned the conversation on the mysterious death of Si-Kaddour. Oh, he affirmed nothing — Simply an allusion to certain secrets that women possess. . . .

Ali had spoken to but one of his friends. As if his words were winged they flew about the *souks*, the *fondouks*, the dwellings. The justice of the *pasha* investigated. The proof of poisoning was lacking; the death of Si-Kaddour had happened more than a year before. Lella Hadra belonged to a powerful family — she was not disturbed. . . .

. . . .

Man's justice is like that of an old blind woman. That of Allah sees all and knows all. He saith, himself, in the Book, " Who digs the pit shall fall therein and who hews the wood will be wounded thereby."

Some months later, Lella Hadra, who had always enjoyed the most perfect health, began to experience strange and cruel pains in her body and limbs. Her abdomen became so enlarged it seemed that of a woman in her ninth month. Her limbs at the same time were covered with frightful ulcers. Her breath was an abomination. Her whole body gave off the effluvia of a corpse.

Old Fatma spread plasters of onion simmered in Arabian butter on the young woman's sores. " Everybody " knows that this is a most efficacious remedy, especially if accompanied by appropriate prayers. But Allah refused his ear to the *surahs* recited for the guilty.

After more than two years of sufferings, great as that of the damned in Gehenna, Lella Hadra died. Ali rejoiced greatly, for he was her heir, and as his was a pious soul, each time that he spoke of his cousin, he whispered in a tone charged with unction.

" She was a great criminal. Allah has punished her."

KHADIDJA'S TWO HUSBANDS

CHAPTER XIII

KHADIDJA'S TWO HUSBANDS

M. Dupont is employed in the Municipal Government of Marrakech. M. Dupont is a lean and kind-hearted little Frenchman with a well-earned reputation for justice.

The natives know this and willingly address their pleas to him. Just a short while ago one of them came to consult him. He was an ex-sharpshooter, a robust chap, about thirty years old, with long plaits against his dark cheeks. The *Medaille Militaire* was pinned to his *djellaba*.

"Who are you?" demanded M. Dupont in the preliminaries.

"Abbes-ben-Mohammed."

"What do you wish?"

"I am just back from France where I was working until the feasts of *Ait-el-kebir*. I had a wife, Khadidja. She remarried while I was gone. Her second husband, Idriss, won't give her back to me."

This is a rather ridiculous and ticklish business, likely to be long drawn out, thought M. Dupont. To settle matters, he attempted a subterfuge.

"Why take back Khadidja? Women aren't so scarce in Marrakech."

M. Dupont spoke in accord with usual native customs. The husband, especially among the lower classes, willingly goes from one woman to another, but Abbes responded,

"It is Khadidja that I want."

"And this Idriss doesn't want to give her back to you?"

"He does not."

"Very well, return with Idriss. When you both are here, we will try to arrange things."

The next day M. Dupont was scarcely installed at his desk, when the *chaouch* announced the first visitor. It was Abbes-ben-Mohammed.

[147]

Khadidja and her second husband accompanied him. The woman was young, scarcely fifteen. As for Idriss, M. Dupont looked at him stupefied. Beneath a brow seamed with deep wrinkles, his eyes were replaced with two empty hollows; a white beard hung on his breast all tangled. He held himself half-bent on his legs, his back hunched, one hand on a stick and an ear cocked in the manner of the sightless.

As a measure of precaution he had twisted his wife's long hair around his wrist and held her fast. Decrepit, filthy, more repulsive, in spite of his infirmity, than pitiable, he formed a striking contrast with his rival whose mighty bulk and rude mien were not without a sort of nobility.

How is it possible, M. Dupont asked himself, for Khadidja to hesitate between the two? —

The contestants lined up before the desk. Idriss continued his hold on Khadidja's hair with his left hand and the woman stood between the two rivals.

Abbes-ben-Mohammed was the first to speak.

" *Sidi*," he said to M. Dupont, " this woman is mine; I have the papers to prove it and I claim her."

The ex-sharpshooter flattered himself he had expressed a strong and irrefutable argument, but the blind man retorted,

" I have papers, too, and they are as good as his. Khadidja is my wife and I keep her."

" She is mine! "

" Dog, thou liest and thy face will go black on the day of judgment! When I married Khadidja she didn't tell me that she was married."

" She should have told you."

" Well, she didn't do it. If a fault has been committed, I have nothing to do with it, and I will not bear the consequences."

Striking the stone floor with his stick to enforce his words, he cried aloud three times,

" She is my wife — she is my wife — she is my wife! "

Infuriated, Abbes-ben-Mohammed attempted to drown the blind man's voice, and throwing out his chest, striking his military medal, he indignantly yelled,

" She is mine — she is mine! "

During all this, between the two husbands, Khadidja remained not only impassive but in the attitude of complete submission that a native woman must observe in the presence of men. The look in her big black eyes, more animal than human, expressed no feeling whatsoever.

M. Dupont was deafened and extremely bored. Here am I like Solomon, he thought, — and yet, I can't cut Khadidja in two —

"Look here," he said, "there must be some way of coming to an agreement!"

The blind man approved. "I ask nothing better. This woman I have fed and clothed for a whole year. Let Abbes-ben-Mohammed pay me back for that and he can have her."

Seeing the trend affairs were taking and understanding at last that the old man intended to turn the argument into a question of *flouss*, the ex-sharpshooter volubly protested,

"May Allah preserve him! I am the one who claims an indemnity! Idriss has made use of my wife for a year. He should pay me damages."

There could never be a similar scene except in a Moslem country. Such haggling would appear to a woman as so cruel an affront to her dignity that she would know immediately what to do; but this was South Morocco, and Khadidja was not one of the more refined women found in the cities. She was a daughter of the *bled*, not long since come from her *douar*. She listened without a tremor, without changing her passiveness by a flicker of the eye.

As for M. Dupont, he was more and more wearied. Hoping to get out of it, he said,

"Listen, go to the *cadi*. This is a question of native customs. I am not competent to handle it."

Together they retired. Believing himself well rid of them at last, M. Dupont rubbed his hands happily together.

Did they go to the *cadi* or did they fail to reach him for lack of a sufficient *fabor* to one of the *Mokhraznis?* Or — which is more probable — were they not satisfied with the judgment when it was rendered? — Anyway, not many days had passed before M. Dupont saw them file again into his office. Abbes still had the same open bearing. The old blind man was not less filthy. Khadidja maintained her animal insensibility and her second husband continued to hold her by the hair.

He who would succeed must be bold. The ex-sharpshooter planted himself first before the desk.

"Well," said M. Dupont, "you have still not come to an understanding?"

"No, *sidi*."

"But it is necessary. Each of you must make some concession."

"It is not possible. I want Khadidja. He wants to keep her; and then he makes a question of *flouss* out of it."

M. Dupont felt discouraged. He looked at Khadidja; he looked at Abbes; he looked at Idriss.

What's to be done? he thought — Unless I settle this thing they will keep coming back every morning —

Suddenly he had an idea. This idea seemed to him so perfect that he was only astonished at not having it sooner. He called the woman up,

"Well, and you? — You have said nothing. Perhaps it is your turn to talk. You are interested in the question in the same way as the others. Whom do you prefer to follow — your first husband, Abbes-ben-Mohammed, or the second, Idriss?"

The woman lifted her head. M. Dupont gazed at her attentively. At last, he thought, we will get out of this mess. . . .

He awaited Khadidja's response curiously, but, as if she dared not speak out, she kept her lips tight closed together. Nothing in her attitude or her look revealed her thought.

M. Dupont was disappointed; then, catching at a last hope,

"Listen, Khadidja, you are frightened and I understand that you cannot decide in such a hurry. You shall think it over. In one week, you'll return, all three. Then you'll tell me what you want to do."

The door closed on them.

Ah! rejoiced M. Dupont — Rid of them for at least a moment. . . .

On the day fixed, with a punctuality altogether exceptional among the natives, M. Dupont saw them reappear. The two husbands had the expansive mien of thoroughly satisfied men.

Abbes-ben-Mohammed spoke,

" We have come to an agreement now."

" Fine," responded M. Dupont. " What have you decided? "

Instead of answering, Abbes replied,

" The blessing of Allah upon thee, *sidi.*" And he repeated, " We have come to an agreement."

M. Dupont understood that it was useless to insist; when a native does not want to tell something, he will not. " Very well, since you are agreed, you have nothing more to seek here."

" The blessing of Allah on thee, *sidi.*"

" Thank you, thank you. Good-by."

Several weeks passed. When M. Dupont chanced to think of the odd contestants who had passed through his office and caused him so much confusion, he said to himself, " Just the same, I'd like mighty well to know which of the two the woman finally preferred. . . ."

It happened that one morning the *chaouch* said to him, " *Sidi*, dost thou remember those goofs that came with that woman — dost know what they did? "

" How should I know? "

" Listen : they went to the keeper of one of those houses where those go who aren't afraid of the fires of hell. She gave them a sum of money which they divided ; they gave her the woman."

" Khadidja? — But — "

" Oh, they are just men. They bought her a pair of *babouches*. She's happy. . . ."

M. Dupont decided that here was a solution that no Westerner would ever have thought of.

HALIMA'S FIRST MARRIAGE

CHAPTER XIV

HALIMA'S FIRST MARRIAGE

Halima has declared herself my friend. Nobody in Marrakech loves me as she does. She takes every chance to insist " Thou art received in the other homes, — they seem to greet thee as I do here, — but it is not the same thing at all. Me, I've known thee a long time. I met thee when thou camest first to the ' Seven Saints ' three years ago. I'm not afraid of thee any more. The others are still afraid. They don't dare to say so but they fear all the French ; they do not yet know quite what they are. But I receive thee with all my heart. Thou art accepted in the other homes but, believe me, it is not so frank a welcome."

While Halima is making me these fond protestations, we are sitting side by side in her own room. The long and very narrow chamber is merely white-washed, but it is luxurious with soft rugs from Rabat and cushions embroidered in silks.

Halima is quite young. Her chief points of beauty are her deep-set eyes and her small teeth, amazingly regular and of a shining whiteness. Oftentimes I amuse myself by saying to her,

" You are so pretty, Halima."

Then she smiles as if I had handed her a mirror ; nestling down among the cushions, her eyes gaze before her, entranced.

She had never known any European women before me. At first her curiosity was trying. She had lifted up the hem of my skirt ; bits of lace had thrown her into an ecstasy. I really believe that I gave her the sheerest happiness of her life when I presented her with a combination of rose crêpe de chine. She gazed at it by the hour, fingering it softly, then locked it away as a most treasured possession in the chest with her scarves.

I do not know by what method and patience, but she had succeeded in making a collection of reproductions from magazines of statues of the Grecian gods in the nude, which she compared in the most unrestrained remarks. She had learned from her husband that this type of conversation was not usual with Europeans, and excusing herself for having shocked me, she would say, " I really didn't know. We see no harm in such things." At present she rarely puts an indiscreet question, or rather, when curiosity impels her, she hesitates first as on a dangerous brink and questions gaily, " Is it something I can say? Is it a thing thou canst speak of? "

Up to now I had always seen Halima wrapped in amply native garments, for which, she says — with a secret desire to dazzle me — the material had never been stinted although it cost dear and is of the finest!

To-day she is in Western clothes which her husband had bought for her in Casablanca — and so much the worse for Halima. Dressed like this she has lost her own special charm ; she has lost the appearance of mystery that her long draperies lent. But I take care not to tell her this and pretend to admire her without end. When she demands, pointing to her new frock, " *kif, kif* (just like) Paris dress? " I assure her, " *kif, kif*."

I add, " Si Ibrahim is a generous husband."

" Oh mother! There is no better husband in Marrakech. And he not only has a big heart — "

She starts up to lift down from the wall an " enlarged " photograph of Si Ibrahim afoot, swathed in his *burnous*. " Isn't he handsome? Every day of my life I thank Allah for divorcing me from my first husband."

She returns to the mattress beside me and we sit cosily together. There are no co-wives to disturb the peace.

Halima is not one of those women who hoard the story of their lives. And how many adventures have already happened in hers. Without forcing them dénouements succeed each other in her history, the vicissitudes tend toward drama. It could really be called a serial romance, successful and yet true.

When Halima married the first time she was still only a lanky little girl trotting through the *souks* for various household purchases or carrying sheets of *kessera* to the public ovens.

" I had no idea," she tells me as we sit together, " of my parents' plans. It is not usual with us to give a husband to a girl who has not yet ' observed Ramadan,' but several times I caught sight of the *g'nafa* coming on a visit. She held long discourses with my mother and whenever she saw me she would begin grinning and calling me her little dove, her baby camel.

" Only a few days later one of our neighbors, Lella Rita, whose husband was a grocer in the *souks*, called on my mother. I fetched in the water for the tea and then went back to my games in the patio. I was near the kitchen, behind a pillar where they could not see me. I overheard my mother and Lella Rita discussing the *sadecq*.

" ' We must have at least one hundred and ten *rei*,' my mother was saying, ' and thou shouldst also throw in a silk *caftan* and an embroidered *ferragiat*.'

" ' A hundred and ten *rei* for such a little girl? — By the Prophet himself, thou seekest to ruin us!' was Lella Rita's tart reply. ' A silk *caftan!* Anyone would think Halima was a *pasha's* daughter. . . . Silk is dear these days. . . .'

" They keep disputing for hours. Suddenly my mother cried, ' If you wish to be stingy with us, we will keep Halima. We'll have no trouble marrying her, ' *Inch Allah!* '

" And then Lella Rita accused my mother of being grasping. Finally, however, they agreed on ninety *rei* and the *caftan*.

" In the days that followed, an old woman whom we sometimes employed for sewing was installed in the house and began working on all sorts of *serouals* and *ferragiats*. She would hold them up and say to me, ' See how beautiful thou wilt be in this.'

" All this time my mother busied herself embroidering cushions and hangings for a new house.

" Visiting neighbors, coming in for tea, kept offering their congratulations, but I was only ashamed. I hid and refused to eat and I cried from Fejer to Acha."

[159]

During the time preceding the nuptials and when the *g'nafa* comes to dress the *arousa* and she is taken to the *hamman* to be purified and anointed with henna, Halima assures me that she cried enough tears to fill a tall pitcher.

The *g'nafa* kept saying, " Thou art lucky. Taher ben Mohammed is both young and handsome. If Allah wills thou canst not but be happy."

But Halima knew that an *arousa* must weep as a sign of good breeding.

Then she adds, to me, " How can I explain to thee, but I was afraid, oh but I was afraid of Lella Rita ; I thought she had an evil look.

" When the moment came for me to leave the house, my poor mother kissed me, ' Forget not that a woman must always please her husband. By the Prophet, thou must do all that Si Taher might desire. Thou must be submissive to Lella Rita — thou must obey her better than thou hast obeyed me. Swear it by Allah and the Prophet. — I wish to hear no evil of thee. . . .' "

In the house of her mother-in-law poor Halima had scant welcome. " That ogress," she cries, speaking of Lella Rita, " had wanted to see her son wed one of her nieces, but her husband had wished otherwise. My marriage had meant the ruin of her plans.

" She blamed me for the whole thing. Oh misery!— She scarcely fed me, she pinched me, she threw pepper in my eyes, turned boiling water over on my feet — and then cursed me for my clumsiness."

There was worse. If it so happens among Moslems that a marriage is celebrated in honor of a very young girl, the union customarily is not consummated until the girl is of marriageable age. But the same evening that Halima entered her mother-in-law's house she became her husband's wife.

" It was for that I could never forgive that daughter of sin," she cries, " and it was because of it I immediately detested Si Taher. During the day I played with the children of the family, my sisters-in-law ; I learned with them to weave wool and crush the grain, but at evening Lella Rita forced me to leave her room where the other children slept and drove me into that of Si Taher."

[160]

Just recalling those dread memories, Halima's eyes harden ; she is shaking all over.

Weeks and months passed. Toward her daughter-in-law Lella Rita remained obdurate, mean and extraordinarily fertile in inventing cruelties. With the tenacity that women, and particularly primitive women, bring to their resolutions, she had made up her mind to make her son detest Halima. What a great day it would be when the little thing was divorced and sent back in shame to her parents. — Allah could create no day more beautiful for her.

The best way to make a woman repulsive to her husband is to make her ugly. He has bought a pretty doll — She must be turned into some sort of monster. — No need to say that such things took place back in the time of witches — they occur in Morocco to-day.

"One day of days," Halima goes on, "my mother-in-law made me a present of something that looked to me like pomegranate peel."

" 'Some friends are coming in after dinner,' she said fawningly, 'friends whom I have especially invited. Eat this — it will make thy teeth pretty.'

" I should have suspected something. Never before had Lella Rita given me anything. Yet I believed her. As I chewed what I supposed to be *souak* (pomegranate peel), I felt my lips, my tongue, and my gums burn as it is said happened to *Beja* in the story where he bit into a pepper pod. I, too, wanted to scream out, 'Fire! Fire!'

" I spat out everything in my mouth, but a few days later my teeth came loose and dropped out one after the other."

Stupefied I raise my head, I stare at Halima and I cry, " Then these that you now have and which I have admired so ? "

The young woman breaks into a long laugh, " Oh fathers, they are false! By my masters, didst thou not guess it? Si Ibrahim had a set made for me at Casa — the blessing of Allah upon him.

" For each tooth that fell out," she resumes, " I cried for hours and I knotted the tooth in my *haik*. The next time my mother came to see me I showed her my gums and my poor fallen teeth. She flew into a passion. A terrific quarrel took place between her and Lella Rita, both of them yelling and casting insults in each other's face. All the neighbors

[163]

were hanging over their roofs to hear better. My mother shouted, 'Thou dog among dogs! It was that stuff you gave her to chew — thou didst it on purpose!'

"'Be still,' yelled my mother-in-law. 'What I gave her was only *souak*, when she says it wasn't, she lies.'

"'Thou art the liar!'

"Finally to bring peace, the neighbors called down, 'Curse Chitane! Curse Chitane!'

"But my mother kept it up, 'I say by the head of the Prophet that it is thou who liest! Some day thou wilt put lice in her *kohl* to blind her, thou wilt put concoctions in her ointment to blacken her skin. . . . I know. . . .'

"'Oh mother! — thou hearest what she dares to imply. May Satan knot thy tongue, thou donkey! I will not even trouble to answer thee. Get out of here or I will take a *djerid* (palm leaf) and drive thee out!'"

During the days that followed, Halima dared not eat or drink.

"My mother had warned me to beware — she thought that Lella Rita might go so far as to poison me. I became as lean and long as a stick, my cheeks hung like empty pouches. I had no strength left. So — my husband divorced me."

"He no longer loved you?"

"Oh he loved me, but he was afraid of his mother. . . ."

Halima begins to speak of something else. It seems I am not to hear how her second marriage to Si-Ibrahim came about. We drink our tea ceremonially. She accompanies me as far as the passageway leading into the street. In a niche in the wall two little slave girls are sitting face to face, their limbs tucked beneath them. They are crushing grain between two grindstones. Their bodies lean forward and they seem to be playing at staring at each other closely, at mirroring each other in their deep dark eyes. Large and high are their head-gears made of red and yellow kerchiefs; on their bare necks shimmer necklaces of bits of brass. Their slim nut-colored arms are bare to the shoulder. I stop near them,

"All is well with thee?"

They smile up at me dumbly.

"What are you thinking about while you work?"

They only hang their heads in terrible shyness.

"What would you expect them to think about?" scoffs Halima fondly.

After shaking hands with me she turns about and returns to her patio. Between these arid walls which enclose her lightsome youth, her one desire, after so many unhappy adventures, is to attain a serene old age. Her husband truly loves her. If it be the will of Allah, even to the end, and without having to share it with another, she will be "mistress of things" in this dwelling.

THE MARRAKECH PRISONS

CHAPTER XV

THE MARRAKECH PRISONS

I wonder what has driven me this morning to seek out the place where justice, according to the *pasha*, is dealt to the people?

It is a vast chamber, its only light coming from the door.   If I should say that its walls are white-washed, I would be saying nothing to distinguish them from all the other native walls.   But in this room a wooden barrier suffices to form a magisterial court.   At one side sit the plaintiffs and the witnesses.   On the other side, on an elevated platform, before a table, are arrayed the *khalifa* of the *pasha*, his judges, and the clerk of the court.

All these gentlemen are in *burnous* or *djellaba*.   A good many of them are considerably astonished to find themselves, for the first time in their lives, not folded on the limbs that Allah has given them, but seated on chairs and benches, those damnable inventions of the West.

There are *Mokhraznis* to maintain order and to introduce the delinquents.   Their red wool bonnets in the form of a pimento pepper, their sharp black eyes and air of uncanny solemnity give them, in my eyes, the appearance of wizards fertile in black magic.   But I am an extravagant creature.   To the initiated the horned and scarlet headdress of the *Mokhraznis* simply means that they are servants of the *Makhzen*.

After one or two young vagabonds, arrested in the *souks* for picking pockets, are tried, a *Mokhrazni* pushes a stolid countryman into the room.   Placed directly before the bar, the fellow turns an indifferent glance on his judges.   There is not a tremor in his expression.   Is it apathy or proud self-control?   The plaintiff arrives.   He is a Berber

[169]

whose black eyes have a squirrel's quick dart. He is the possessor of sheep flocks in the *bled*, watched over by nomad children.

It is a simple case. The guilty man had confessed. He had stolen a sheep; he had disposed of it for a hundred francs.

But before the judges he begins to deny it. As firm on his big feet as a column on its base, he repeats stubbornly,

" I have always kept to the straight and narrow path."

Attentive but unconvinced the *khalifa* listens, caressing his white beard with a round, well-cared-for hand weighted down on the little finger with a silver ring where a diamond shines.

" *Ia*," he interrupts, " but thou hast confessed thyself to have stolen. . . ."

" If I said that I didn't know what I was talking about. *Mellah* Jews had filled me up with wine. . . ."

" What have you done with the money? "

" I have no money. Allah, Allah! — I am a *meskine*."

" Be silent. Thou liest — "

The *khalifa* makes a sign to the *Mokhrazni*. With a turn of the wrist the man is despoiled of his *djellaba;* the dirty rag around his head is twisted off. Poll shaven, head hanging, he stands with only a single *gandourah* left to him, about his shoulders a vest which must have been ravishingly pretty when it was new. It is strawberry color with a lining of green. Soutache is braided in a vermicelle pattern across the fronts.

The *Mokhrazni* rips the buttons with one jerk of a brutal hand. He feels over the faded stuff. Then from the lining, one after the other, he triumphantly draws out a bill of twenty francs, one of five, and a two sous piece.

Cherifian justice is swift in its movements. There and then the money is restored to the plaintiff who is perfectly satisfied with the little rose vest lined with green.

He takes the bills, stuffs them in his money bags at once; just as he is slipping in the two sous piece, a remembrance of pity softens him. He hands the coin to the thief.

" Here, take it, brother. . . ."

But what is this he hears? The *khalifa* condemns the prisoner to six months in prison. Only six months in prison for stealing a sheep! Is it possible? Our man whirls around, marches back to the bar.

"*Sidi*, that's not enough. By Allah! Six months! My sheep was a huge sheep! *Sidi*, I entreat thee, condemn him to at least a year. Soon as he gets out, you wait and see, he'll do it again. . . ."

With a wearied air the small white hand of the *khalifa* fans the air. "Enough, enough!"

The *Mokhraznis* push the condemned man before them from the room. Another prisoner is brought in and the owner of the sheep, having hidden the rose vest with its pretty lining in his *djellaba*, resignedly departs.

The last case called is that of a woman, Khadidja ben Omar.

She enters in an indolent pace. Under the heavy woolen tissue of her *haik* her shoulders are bent and nothing of her face is visible except the glistening line of her eyes above the woolen band.

A "daughter of joy," she uses the money she makes to buy *kohl*, clothes, perfumes; in spite of the Prophet's law, sometimes she adds alcohol to her purchases. The week before, being tipsy, she had made an uproar in the *souks*.

A *Mokhrazni* had arrested her. When he threatened her with the anger of the seven saints who protect the city, she had answered, she had dared to answer —

"May the seven saints, yes, even they, go to — "

Imagine a similar scene in France in the twelfth and thirteenth centuries. In that day and time they burned men who said no more than that.

Khadidja had been thrown into prison. To-day, humiliated, contritely sober, her big mouth silent, she droops before the reproving faces of the *khalifa* and his judges.

As numerous and vehement as if nothing less than a murder were at stake, the witnesses file past. Crouched over his paper, the court clerk takes down each deposition without losing a word.

In the meantime the judges discuss among themselves the fitting sentence to decree. The *khalifa*, who is strong for the punishments

[173]

meted out in the old days, says ceremoniously that for such a crime as that they used to cut off both wrists — and it was not too much.

At which, the French officer present on the platform thinks it time to intervene. Khadidja is condemned to fifteen days in prison. Solemn in their white *burnous*, under their open veils, the judges dare not protest. The last word, in everything, goes to the French. Allah has willed it thus, but each of them is thinking, it is plain to see, that we make strange judges. We have introduced Pity at the bar of justice. That lady was never seen there in the days of the ancient *Makhzen*.

Then for a mere peccadillo they cut off the feet or the wrists, they burst the eyeballs, they snatched out the tongue ; and, going back into his near-by palace, the *pasha* could feel that at least he had not wasted his day.

One of the *Mokhraznis* leads Khadidja from the room. Knowing that this woman, whose case I had heard tried, was going to serve her sentence in one of the city prisons, I was seized with the notion to visit them.

In order to do it I had to wait several days until the authority, requested at Rabat, should reach me.

The prisons of Marrakech have been installed in the ruins of the " Golden " Sultan's palace.

It is easily seen how Moulay-Ahmed deserved this ostentatious surname. He was the most powerful of all the Saadian sultans. He was a courage-hardy creature who never ceased his warfare. After clearing the coast of Spaniards and Portuguese, he threw himself into the conquest of the Soudan. War then was not as saintly as its name.

The Soudanese were Moslems like the Moroccans, but they were rich. Moulay-Ahmed picked a quarrel with them. Knowing that they were obliged to come in the region of Marrakech to buy the slabs of salt necessary to their feeding, arguing that, in the name of the Prophet, he was their religious head, he pretended to exact from them a gold piece as a salt tax.

This the Soudanese refused point-blank. The sultan of Morocco marched against their sovereign. It is difficult to conceive of the efforts represented by such an expedition, in such an epoch, in such a climate.

In the first place it was necessary to scale the sharp peaks of the Atlas with camels and mules. These beasts, their forefeet slipping, would drag the men who led them into the precipices gaping on either side. The mountains once cleared, the desert opened its yellow embrace.

It was four and a half months of harrying march, bringing everything with them, food and arms, before they arrived at the gold-filled country, at Timbuctoo, the great Black City.

The *harkas* of the sultan were innumerable and they were armed with guns. The emperor of the Soudan was vanquished. What could his soldiers avail with their lances and javelins?

Moulay-Ahmed, called the Victorious, returned in triumph to his kingdom. When he reentered the gates of Marrakech, escorted by his *harkas*, he brought home so much gold, so many jewels and ingots, that his dazzled people renamed him *El Deheli*, the Golden.

This sultan employed his fabulous riches in constructing a palace whose like had never before been seen. It was baptized the Marvel.

Expense was forgotten. The most dexterous workmen were called in from every country. Marbles were bought in Italy. By sea, as ballast, they came as far as Tangiers. From there, camel-back and man-back — after how many days of march — they reached Marrakech. A mere bagatelle was written large on the expense account. Nothing was used except what was reputed the best of its kind. Lime was brought from far-off Timbuctoo. An order from the sultan, and the desert's immensity was abolished.

The palace walls lifted in the dry, clear air. They covered eighty acres and were made of bricks rosy with the soil of Marrakech. The salons were decorated in a richness beyond description. All the capitals of the supporting columns were plaques of gold ; the Koran inscriptions that ran along the walls were of gold ; the platforms of cedar wood were inlaid with gold. Everywhere glistened onyx and marble.

Of this palace which the "Golden" constructed and of which, say the Arab poets, " the gazelle was so jealous that she lost her beauty," nothing remains but an immensity of ruin. In that part which has most resisted time, the city has installed its prisoners.

A dust-thick esplanade prolonged from a passageway bordered on either side with old walls whose decorations are crumbling, a door under a high arch that has fallen in, a little staircase with wooden treads, and I enter a monumental vestibule with rounded Moorish arches.

To my left, the sentry who is my guide assures me, there is an immense and mysterious chamber.

"Its walls, which are more than a yard thick, madame, have no opening. Not in the sides or in the roof. I've looked everywhere."

"What does it enclose, does anybody know?"

"Some say that there are skeletons in there — those of the members of his family whom the "Golden" wished to get rid of. Others will assure thee that in that room, the sultan had hoarded up his secret treasure. It must still be full of gold and precious stones. . . ."

On the heels of my guide and with a spirit crammed with his dazzled imaginings, I come into an immense court. There, once were laid out the sultan's fresh green *riadhs* (gardens) with alleys of tile. Four excavations mark the spot of vanished basins, corresponding in symmetry, that were set down the center.

To-day it abounds in brambles. On a little mound stands a palm tree; it alone has succeeded in pushing through the deserted waste.

By the destructive efforts of man and centuries, the marble pillars have been disjointed, the squares of precious ceramics have been broken. Nothing is left that once made these *riadhs* gardens of delight.

Coming out from the arid courtyard, between two high walls of crushing height, I arrive at a little patio surrounded by the structures which are still standing. Their roofs are in fissures, rain-water disintegrates them, humidity corrodes. The one of the four chambers less dilapidated than the others is used to imprison those condemned by the justice of the *pasha*.

How many are there? A dozen more or less. I come on them clothed only in gray smocks, crammed into the one corner that is warmed by the sun. An old sentry armed with a strap suffices to guard them.

Where is Khadidja ben Omar? She is pointed out to me. This "daughter of joy," I might say, is not beautiful. "Daughters of joy" rarely are. It is just as well that they leave something to honest women.

What is the prison régime? Khadidja, as well as her companions, already has flabby flesh with a grayish cast upon it. When I ask her, through the *arifa* (guard), how she had dared to blaspheme the " seven saints," she responds,

" It was written above — "

When one reasons thus, one is not encumbered with repentance. That would be superfluous.

On the other side of the passageway, a sentry opens the men's prison for me. It is impossible to tell what part of that old-world palace this once was used for.

A gallery circles an immense court ; on it give the various cells. The prisoners are grouped in them by category.

The sentry takes one of the keys from his great key-ring. The key grinds in the lock, the door gives.

Little boys of twelve to fifteen leap to their feet staring toward me with batting eyelids because the vivid light of day, coming so suddenly, had dazzled them.

Why are criminals always represented with base or vicious faces? These little fellows, whom vice has already deeply touched, show in their naïve faces that caressing glance, alive with tenderness, which so many of their race have, a glance that melts the heart.

Expecting that their evening meal was being brought to them, at first they were disappointed ; then, from seeing that I had been able to get in to see them, they jumped to the conclusion that I must be the wife of some powerful personage in the " French *Makhzen*." They held toward me their supplicating hands, they began to beg me to procure them their liberty.

The sentry pushed them roughly inside. Alas ! I could do nothing for them — and even if I had been able to, what inscrutable reasons would have opposed themselves to my request.

For those with a feeling heart it is best not to go into prisons where there are children. . . .

The hour has come for the adult prisoners to take their exercise. They walk one behind another in the big courtyard. Under the blue sky, in the clear air, they form an immense grayish circle where *burnouses* alternate with prison-striped *djellabas*.

[177]

Some of them wear a glance of mournful resignation, like captive birds ; but most of them lope along indolently with uncaring faces ; around they turn under the eye of the sentry ; they turn like a flock of brutes and some of them are indeed as brutal as beasts: that one there, for example, who in the same evening killed his wife, his daughter and his mother-in-law, and who sniggers, throwing a sly glance toward us, because he guesses that they are telling me about him and his crime.

My guide has lighted an acetylene lamp. By a rude staircase we descend into the vaults.

No, nothing, nothing on earth can give an idea of the terror they cast upon the soul. It is a frightful experience to view the prisons of the past.

These had served exactly up to the time that the French had taken dominion at Marrakech. There the *pasha* had packed together those he had condemned. The guide affirms that when the French abolished the subterranean vaults the prisoners in them numbered more than four thousand.

Under the ghastly acetylene light the vaulted arches range around us, passageways hollow out their sinister depths ; the glance is lost in an abyss — a black that is absolute blackness. Caves open out of the walls ; sepulchres where never a thread of sunlight enters.

In the past there was not even a door that could be opened. Simply a hole in the wall, just big enough for a man to squeeze through. His head was pushed in before him.

And what a silence in these catacombs!

The ones who were chained within could yell their grief aloud ; there was no danger of its being heard by happier men who, above their heads, drank in the pure and liberal air spiced with garden flowers.

Cherifian justice could not be bothered with feeding those it imprisoned. Those who had relatives and succoring friends received food. The others got nothing. The demoniac scenes that have unrolled in these entrails of a palace! The frightful battles for a drop of water, a taste of *kessera!*

My guide has words to freeze me : " The famishing ate each other. . . ."

As if this was not enough of what I came to see, he had me mount a platform where the condemned was suspended by an iron collar about his neck so that the bottoms of his struggling feet were wounded by sharp-pointed swords.

It might be objected, " But that was a question of great criminals."

Ah, indeed I am not so sure about that. Too often I am surer of the contrary. Numbers of those enclosed within these subterranean walls were honest men. It was their misfortune to possess a portion of land, a bit of silver that excited the envy of one more powerful than they and they would not cede it.

In any case, guilty or innocent, the captives of these jails were men and I know that when a man comes to die, it is unbelievable that it should be necessary to torture him a long time beforehand.

AN EVENING WITH SI TAHER
BEN MOHAMED

CHAPTER XVI

AN EVENING WITH SI TAHER
BEN MOHAMED

For more than five minutes Mme. D— and I had been standing in front of Si Taher's house, waiting for someone to open the door to us. In vain we had carefully knocked the consecrated three raps on the portal. No voice from within responded, " *Askoun?* (who is there?) " and the porter was still invisible.

And yet the engagement had been made only yesterday for Si Taher to introduce us to " the house." The " master of things " had even had the affability to ask us to stay to supper. Turning toward me he had given us advice which had much amused me though I tried to hide it. " Don't eat too much at thy hotel. — The cooking is good at my house. . . ."

" Knock one more time," said Mme. D—, who had reached the end of her patience. " After that, if they don't hear us, we'll go on."

The panels resound under our palms. Ah! At last! There is the faint sound of a voice deep within. Confusedly we get,

" Oh misery, it is the madames! Si Taher has gone out! "

" Open the door! "

" We're locked in. The darky is not there. Have ye been waiting long? — Wait just a little longer. The darky will be back. . . ."

Just then he makes an effective entrance at the corner of the alley. He is adorned with a huge ring of keys like a prison-keeper, those of all the doors of the house. Beneath a pale bluish *caftan* whose light shade strikingly contrasts with the deep ebon of his skin, he advances insolently through the alley.

[183]

" Blessing of Allah on thee! " exclaims Mme. D— in exasperation. " Where have you been? You didn't mind keeping us waiting. . . ."

As one who has no explanations to furnish — unless to his master — the black growls that he was at his prayers. We might consider ourselves lucky that he consented to interrupt them for *Roumiyas*. . . .

We cross the threshold past the door swung back at last on its hinges. Before us between two high walls narrow passages open into each other at right angles. Several small compartments in these passageways receive light from the one opening, the door. There the servants live or the " clients " of Si Taher when they come in to spend a few days at Marrakech on business from the *bled*.

One of this sort of huts is open. Under the direction of a ruler held by an old teacher wrapped in a dirty cloak, a row of children are swaying their bodies to the chants of the Koran. How many are there seated side by side in the same dust, in a fine half-light that would have delighted the heart of Rembrandt? I manage to count five. They are the young sons of Si Taher and this is their private school. That they are about the same age, that there are only two or three months between several of them might seem at first astonishing, but there is nothing surprising about it, after all, in this country.

A final door opens into further passages and at last the patio appears with its arcaded galleries. Certainly since I have been in Morocco I have seen many patios — but not one of them is like another. They have their own personality to awaken interest and pique the visitor's curiosity. There have been some that I remember only with terror — their dreariness, their imprisonment. Colored in turquoise and emerald, this one of Si Taher's arouses a true enchantment.

Between the tiny shining squares that cover the floor and the deep azure sky exists a luminous symphony of color that rises upward and redescends and whose brilliance is tempered by the green shade of tree branches. The proud, high stems of lush banana plants spring from deeply sunk beds. The bunches of ripening fruit hang their amber crescents to be gilded in the sun-rays ; a stream of water sings in a marble basin. All the magic charm of distant lands is prisoned within four walls.

Si Taher finally rejoins us in one of the long halls. Neither big nor little, he is the common type of stout Moroccan. In a very few years the sedentary city life produces the true bourgeois of pudgy cheeks and fat paunch.

My open admiration for his patio flatters one of his weak points, but it would be too like the new-rich to show it, to agree, " Yes, it is beautiful."

Putting on a modest air, Si Taher protests largely, " *Ia*, madame, this one at my house is small, tiny even. It is nothing to compare with the one at the *pasha's*."

" What do you mean? Your patio is absolutely perfect."

" The patio of a poor man!"

" You a poor man. — You a *meskine!* "

" Certainly."

" You are joking."

" *Ia*, madame, we are all *meskines*. Some beg in the streets from the passers-by ; some beg directly of God."

" Well, I prefer to be among the latter."

My host lifts pious eyes to the sky, then without a shadow of irreverence, but with a sly twinkle, he responds,

" Thou art right — one is likely to get more from there."

How rapidly Morocco is striding over boundaries. How quick its people are to assimilate our method and manners. Si Taher's father in all his long life never quitted the city of " Seven Saints." His son — well, his son has been up in an airplane. A great traveler, quite unafraid of distance, last year he even visited America. He took one of his sons along as interpreter and secretary ; on their return trip they went through the principal cities of France.

I ask, " Did you make such a long journey on business? "

" No, only to see, only to delight my eyes."

" Ah, when one has money —! "

The supper hour has not yet arrived. The *tagines* are still perhaps simmering on the native *kanouns*. Let us go in and meet " the home."

Aside from a few rugs on the floor there is no luxury in the room we enter. Beside Lella Jolikha sits Fatima, one of the master's favorite slaves. They both have an air of weariness and their eyes turn toward us darkly circled.

" Are you ill? " asks Mme. D—.

" Ill? By Allah, no, but it will soon be *Ramadan* and we have fasted the entire day."

" You mean you are beginning before the ' sacred month ' ? "

My complete ignorance of some of their customs makes my hostess smile. " I see you do not know about these things. You see, one can never keep the entire fast of *Ramadan*. There are days when one is so tired one gives out. So before beginning another *Ramadan* one must fast for the days still owing."

" Hadn't you all year for that? "

" Oh fathers, yes. But thou knowest how prone one is to say, ' To-morrow — I will do it to-morrow. . . .' Then the last days come around and one has to get it over with."

In the meantime we have all seated ourselves. Fatima's face is not at all pretty but quite pert and humorous. In order to prove to me that she is not so unsophisticated, she tells me that last year she made a trip to France herself. " And, madame, I was dressed just like you, a hat, a dress and little shoes, that I couldn't even walk in."

What she says seems so impossible that I do not believe a word of it; but Mme. D— assures me, " Fatima was not well; Si Taher, who loves her very much, sent her to a European spa because the doctors advised it."

" When you arrived in Marseille, what was it that astonished you most, Lella Fatima? "

At first she murmurs timidly, " I don't know," for she has more animation than reflection, then she thinks a moment,

" It was to see all the men walking about unarmed. In Marrakech each one carries his poignard."

I attempted to explain to Fatima the French police organization, but she does not understand and besides, that does not interest her.

She starts off again volubly, " I've been to Lyon and to Paris, too. Paris! — The Bois de Boulogne is such a pretty *bled* — Why dost thou smile? "

Fatima did not feel shy in France very long. After the first few days she never noticed whether people stared or not. Before that she felt what she calls, " shame of the face." A Frenchwoman to whom she had an introduction went about with her. — " I went into all the shops and to the cinema. . . ."

" And then when you came back to Marrakech and were again shut in by your veil —? "

" One must enjoy nice things while one has them and not think of them when Allah takes them away."

There are other women who are not so reasonable as Fatima. Of finer natures perhaps, their feelings are deeper than hers, and I can think of many a one who came back as she did to the restrictions of the harem and pined for the taste they had had of freer living and never really recovered from that one glimpse they had got of an open door. . . .

As might be expected, Fatima's trip did not fail to arouse her mistress' envy. On a " day of days " Lella Jolikha intends to get to France in her own turn — if God wills ; but, she adds disdainfully, she will not go alone, " sent off like a sack of sweet potatoes," — Si Taher will go with her.

" In the meantime," murmurs the other maliciously, " he goes off to America and leaves you at home. . . ."

" What do you do while he is gone? " asks Mme. D—. " You weep and mourn? "

" Heavens, if I were to weep every time he goes away I would have neither eyes nor eyelids left — my tears would have worn a channel down my cheeks ! "

While we have been talking a tiny boy, very dark-skinned but dressed in European fashion, has been whirling around and around the patio in a toy automobile. Mme. D— calls to him. Instead of answering, the child speeds up his doughty car. After a moment he bursts into the room at full speed, guides it over the rugs, and threatens the safety of our life and limbs.

" Come, Si Ali," coaxes Lella Jolikha, " come and say good-day."

He is not very enthusiastic about the procedure, but at last consents to come up to us. What is his place in the household? One of the master's sons evidently, but which mother? —

Mme. D—, whom I ask, responds in French, " His mother is a slave."

" Lella Jolikha has no child? "

" No, and it breaks her heart."

" Is she afraid her husband will divorce her? "

" She is of a fine family and he would not dare put such an affront upon them, but she knows that it irritates him to see that children are born to him by all his slaves. The only woman who fails to give him one is his legitimate wife."

In the meantime the little fellow has gone to hide himself in a corner of Lella Jolikha's *caftan*. She pets him gently and murmurs childish love-names, " My little steed — my little lion. . . ."

She has guessed that my friend and I were talking about the child and her, and she says,

" I love him like my own son. Last year he was very sick and I nursed him. I was so terrified lest he should die that I almost died myself. She that had brought him into the world showed no uneasiness. Of the two of us it was easily seen which was the true mother."

A slave crosses the patio, brilliant in a mandarin-colored robe. Seeing us there, her dark face lights with a flash of white enamel. Just a few years ago her mother, torch high in her hand, served as light-bearer. She simply presses an electric switch. The shadow of iron bars instantly stripes the white-washed wall that faces the door and the narrow windows.

The supper-hour approaches. Si Taher comes to hunt us, Mme. D— and myself. We return to that lovely patio, conceived in a festive spirit by some unknown architect who had placed all his talents at the service of felicity.

Four dishes are set in a row in the doorway, four hooded dishes. The first, I know, contains mutton with carrots, if not with sweet potatoes. The second contains, not less surely, mutton with sweet potatoes, unless it be with carrots. In the third, I would wager my head at the stake, there is mutton with chick-peas, and in the fourth, I can as surely affirm there will be *couscus, couscus* which I do not like but which I shall pretend to enjoy, as I was taught in childhood that well-bred people eat everything set before them and I am abominably well-bred.

When the meal with all its ceremonies was ended, Mme. D— and I were about to leave, but Si Taher detained us. He had ordered a clown, in the manner of the old lords, to furnish us amusement.

This fellow is a darky. During the day one might think him only a simple mason, but with the coming of evening he will be whatever you might wish, a " madame," a *tajer*, a beggar or even a simple animal.

" Who taught you all this, Ahmed? "

" No one, madame."

In the opening of the door this odd son of Cham plants himself solidly on his bare legs, his smock cut off to the knee. A *rezza* is wound amply around his head. Behind him, for a drop-curtain, hangs the purple-black night and the domed banana plants with their lustrous leaves.

He begins to act. Entirely alone, he sketches a group of people for us, a Frenchwoman first, traveling with her husband and her little pug-dog.

Ahmed knows no French, but he has noticed every gesture of the tourists, has remembered a few of their phrases, and can reproduce each inflection.

The lady walks slowly along. We can see her. She is small, a bit stout, short-legged. She has a reticule, a lorgnette and a " loulou " dog.

He trots along beside her, " wow, wow, wow. . . ."

The husband follows, hands in his pockets, thoughts elsewhere.

Suddenly the " loulou " is lost.

Madame turns on monsieur, " I tell you it is all your fault! "

Monsieur protests, " How? How? "

With her lorgnette madame peers into the four corners of the square Djaa el F'na, shrieking in high falsetto, " Doggie, doggie, doggie — here, here! "

His strong arms outside his *gandouras*, Ahmed stretches into the empty air hands that would fell an ox. By what miracle do we suddenly realize that these enormous paws are dimpled little hands kept white with beauty-creams? By what other miracle do we see the little dog run up, hear his squeals, his low moans and whimpers for fear of being beaten? No one could tire of watching Ahmed's amazing gestures, of studying on his animal-like face an ever-changing mimicry that is exact in every step.

[191]

The fat lady stoops with difficulty ; she gathers the " loulou " into her arms. " There, there, bad darling. Mamma's little bitsy dear — "

She moves on. Behind her her husband puffs and shrugs his shoulders.

A minute's entr'acte and we are in the *souks* with a shoemaker who is mending some *babouches*. His *rezza* over one ear, the good old fellow hammers his leather, draws his thread, stretches it, knots it. *Babouche* in the air, he inspects it from the side. Is it a good job? No. — He shakes his head and begins over, humming a little song of his own composition,

" Just a bit of bread and butter nearby to delight me. . . .
Just a pigeon with pimentos, a stuffed chicken nearby to delight me. . . .
Just a singing bird, a scented spring of jasmin, a glass of tea beside me for my great delight. . . ."

Appears the native police agent to claim the citizen's tax. " Ahmed ben Ali, No. 16? — Thou art the man. You owe forty francs, fifty centimes. . . ."

Not by inspiration but because men have recourse to the same ruses in all countries and in all climates when they try to repudiate their debts, the good shoemaker begins to play the madman.

You might believe you were listening to *L'Agnelet* in the *Farce de Maitre Parhelin*. He answers every word put to him with a silly laugh.

" Ass's head, don't you understand anything? " shouts the agent. " Forty *francs*, fifty *centimes*. . . . You don't want to understand? — Just wait a minute. I'm going to get the French agent."

The latter comes on the scene. He is small and thin and whistles an ancient soldier-ditty,

" Aupres de ma blonde
Qu'il fait bon, fait bon. . . ."

His booklet open before him, he talks himself blue in the face. He menaces in a deep rumble — fines, imprisonment. . . . Then he walks off again and for another instant we hear,

" Aupres de ma blonde,
Qu'il fait bon, fait bon. . . ."

[192]

the whistle diminishing to indicate that the Frenchman is far, far away.

Then the wily shoemaker tugs gently at a corner of the agent's *djellaba*, " By the Prophet I'll treat thee to a glass of coffee if thou wilt grant me a further delay. . . ."

" Why the devil didst thou not say it sooner, brother? I'd have been spared the trouble of going after the Nazarene. . . ."

Ahmed disappears. After just long enough time to give himself a fat belly with stuffed cushions, he reappears, to us and to himself, a portly notable of Fez. Ah, the important bearing of a man with coffers full of *flouss !* Squatting before an imaginary *tagine* Ahmed grubs around in it with three delicate fingers ; between bites we hear unmannerly noises whose incongruity shocks every well-brought-up Moroccan, but which give rise to innumerable quips against the Fascis.

The evening's performance ends with a domestic quarrel among natives out on the *bled.* The husband, who has been to the nearest village, tramps peacefully home to his *douar.* His wife is waiting for him.

An impressive greeting is ready for him at the threshold — a respectful kiss on the hem of his *burnous.* " Greetings, lord. All is well with thee ? "

" All is well."

" Where is the cottonstuff that thou didst promise to buy me ? "

" By Allah ! — I hadn't the time for it. I'll do it next trip."

" Next time? Oh daughter of my master, thou hearest him ? Oh misery, what sort of a husband have I fallen to ? He gives me no henna, no scarves, no perfumes, no cotton-stuff to make me a *caftan !* "

There is a melodramatic scene of despair. The woman moans, interrupted by sobs,

" I won't stay here any longer ! . . . I'm leaving now ! . . . I know where to go to get something to eat. . . . I'm going back to my people. . . . I'm going back to my father. . . ."

An old, very decrepit crone arrives on the scene. Her spine is bent, her head palsied ; she coughs and dodders, all her teeth are missing and we barely hear what she says — which is a pity, for she is full of good advice,

" Thou weepest, foolish little one ! Thou weepest because thou hast no henna and new clothes ! In my day women had more patience. Thou wouldst return to thy father ? . . . Allah bless thee, but thinkest thou thy father wants thee? Thinkest thou he will be glad to feed thee, to return thy dowry? — Foolish, foolish girl — stay with thy husband. . . ."

But the young woman is still obdurate. While she seems to turn her spindle, to weave the thread through her bony old fingers, the crone chants on with creaking voice and shaking head,

" Everything was different when I was young. Everything was better, everything was much better. We worked faster ; we knew how to wash wool and spin it. We respected our husbands, we were afraid of them. When they made us 'eat of the stick,' we kissed their hands and cried, 'Thou art right, lord, thou art right. . . .' Things were better than this day and time."

THE LITTLE SHEPHERDESS OF THE ATLAS

CHAPTER XVII

THE LITTLE SHEPHERDESS OF THE ATLAS

Could it be the sonorous name of Azrou that attracts me? Are the great cedar forests wafting toward me their mysterious appeal? — I feel pounding in my veins the happy fever of voyagers. On to the future! On to the unknown! — Ah, how well I understand La Fontaine's shepherd who "sold his flock to embark on an adventure."

It has rained during the night and the sky is still laden with swollen, menacing clouds. A cold wind that envelops the railway carriage assails us first on one side, then on the other. Hard to imagine that if the sun were shining on this same route we would be suffering from unbearable heat.

Before us are great rocks in upright cliffs of a shiny black with a sinister glint. Only when we come quite close do they reveal their true color. Gray, a saddening gray, with large rusty slabs, they disclose deep fissures which nomads inhabit.

There is little light even though it lacks but two hours to midday. The Morocco which I am plunging into is that which Loti knew in the same season ; damp and cold.

Every little while huge trucks pass us. Laden with long cedar beams, they are coming down from the great forests of the Atlas and leave in their passage a penetrating and homely odor of freshly cut wood.

We move rapidly by the village of El-Hajeb perched upon a peak of the mountain. In the pile of rocks a few black nanny goats are climbing the perpendicular sides. Boy or girl, some child is watching them. Thin with a hunger never satisfied, clothed in a dirty rag that means no protection against the cold, they excite the compassion of the tourists as they pass.

[199]

There was once, in this region at Ben-Ahmed, one of these small shepherdesses who presented herself before the *cadi*. It seemed so unreasonable that a little creature of her class should have business with a personage such as the *cadi*, that the *Mokhrazni* on guard stopped her at the door.

" What is it you want? "

With complete assurance the infant responded,

" To see the *cadi* himself."

The *Mokhrazni* let her pass. Waiting her turn, the little thing went to crouch beside a sun-warmed wall. She was almost bare, but around her head, secured with a string, she had carefully adjusted a veil of blue cotton. As though modesty demanded it, the ends of the faded stuff hid her hair, fell over her narrow shoulders, and revealed to the curious only the tiny tip of a nose, the curve of a brown cheek and two large, very grave eyes.

She had not been squatting there less than three hours when the *Mokhrazni* finally turned toward her :

" Your turn."

He pushed her toward the *cadi*. Seated on his mat, clothed in a *caftan* of that barely bluish tone which the natives affect and which they call " sugary," draped, in addition, in the white depths of his *burnous*, the *cadi* was an old man whose flowing white beard lent him an air of smiling majesty.

He raised his head and paternally regarded the small solicitor.

The Moroccans, so hard on animals, and, oftentimes, on each other, have a great tenderness for children.

Gently, in a grave voice he questioned her,

" What is thy name, little child? "

" Aïcha ben-Mohammed."

" Where is thy father? "

" In the bosom of Allah."

" Thy mother? "

" *Kif, kif.*"

" With whom dost thou live? "

The *cadi* waited for her to answer, " With my elder sister, with my brother, with my grandparents — " But in a forthright tone she announced,

" With my husband."

" Thou? Thou hast a husband? "

" It was the will of Allah."

" Since when? "

" Since the feast of *Mouloud*."

The *cadi* calculated and found that this was eight months since.

" Who is thy husband? " he went on.

" Mustapha-ben-Ibrahim."

" The water-carrier in the *souks?* "

" The same."

" And he sent you to me? "

" No, *sidi*."

" Then why didst thou seek me? What dost thou want? "

Without a shadow of hesitation the little thing replied,

" To tear the card."

Half seriously, half ironically, for the gravity of the child amused him, the *cadi* continued :

" Thou hast sufficient ground to divorce thy husband? "

" Yes, *sidi*. He beats me."

" Thou canst not only say it, thou must prove it."

" Look — "

As she spoke Aïcha displayed her little legs, her arms, her thin back on which the long bruises appeared still bloody.

" Allah, Allah," cried the *cadi*, " if thou didst that which is agreeable to Mustapha-ben-Ibrahim, if thou hadst stayed in the straight path, without turning to the right nor the left, thou wouldst not ' eat of the stick.' Go back to thy husband, Aïcha, and do better. Come, out with you — "

The child made a grimace of vexation but she did not budge.

" *Sidi*," she said, drawing herself up to her full small height, " *sidi*, listen — I have not told thee all. He has married me and I have not yet observed *Ramadan*."

The *cadi* ceased to smile. The *chraa* forbids the possession of a girl before she has reached marriageable age.

" What thou hast declared is very grave," he said. " Stay here. Our matrons will see if thou hast told the truth."

[203]

The divorce was pronounced. Very few formalities for that — A phrase scribbled by the *cadi's* secretary on the back of the marriage " card " and Aïcha regained her freedom.

Except for a brother a year older than she and a shepherd like herself, the child had no relative. What was to be done with her? Beneath the old scrap of tarpaulin that imperfectly covered her, showed a hollow stomach, a fleshless back, arms and legs that looked like sticks.

The *cadi* reflected for a few moments, then Allah sent an inspiration. There was then at Ben-Ahmed, the household of a young Nazarene official. He had a baby two years old. Perhaps he would take charge of Aïcha as a nursemaid for the child. — With them, the little girl would be well treated and well nourished.

The *cadi* wrote a note to the Nazarene. On the same day Aïcha took the place that had been provided for her.

Bathed, cleaned of lice by Fatma, one of the servants, dressed in proper clothes, shod in *babouches* that plunged her into intense admiration, and with a " warm stomach " by grace of a good meal — Aïcha experienced a happiness that seemed to her without end.

" Oh my fathers," she cried to Fatma, " Aïcha — thou seest how Aïcha is now *kif, kif* a daughter of *tajers!* "

Docile to the orders given her, patient and sweet with the little fellow she nursed, the child attached herself to her masters. She had only one fault — she was greedy. — Not so reprehensible when one is only eight.

Carried away by the good eating, Aïcha regaled herself not only with what Fatma, the cook, gave her, but with all she could pinch from the store-room besides. The result followed shortly. She was seized with terrific indigestion. For forty-eight hours she was put on a diet and her mistress, Mme. C—, gave her a long sermon on the inconveniences of greediness which Aïcha listened to submissively.

" Oh my mother," she cried penitently, " thou art right. . . . Aïcha is only a dog . . . she is not worthy of thy kindness! "

But when she was alone with Fatma, the child grumbled, " It was what they gave me to eat that made this *baroud* (warfare) in my stomach — and now they are going to let me die of hunger. . . ."

Aïcha had been with her mistress exactly one week when, entering the kitchen in the early morning, the servant, Fatma, received a shock. On the tile floor, near the door, all the linen and clothing given to Aïcha lay carefully folded. Beside them, toe to toe, sat the *babouches*, the little new *babouches* whose possession had given the infant such joy.

Fatma went to the room where Aïcha slept. The child was not there. Beyond a doubt she had run away. — Run away or been stolen, perhaps, by some native who had noticed her growing beauty.

Mme. C— called one of the *Mokhraznis* attached to the regional bureau and placed the matter in his hands.

"Yes," said he, "— a little girl — thin legs — Rest easy — she won't be far. I'll go on my horse and overtake her."

Toward the end of the morning he reappeared. As if she were a grand criminal, he clutched the weeping child by the shoulder.

When she saw Mme. C— her tears redoubled and she cast herself on her knees.

"Indulgence! Indulgence!" she cried. "Why hast thou sent for me? Aïcha is no thief. I left everything thou gavest me. . . . Why dost thou make them send me to prison?"

"My poor child," cried Mme. C— pityingly, "I don't want them to punish you. I only wanted to know what had become of you. Tell me why you ran away. Didn't you like it here?"

"I liked it so much. Thou art my mother and little Jean is my brother — I would cut off my flesh to keep him from harm."

"Yet you ran away from us. Why?"

Instead of answering, the child stood with hanging head. Finally to make her speak, Mme. C— appealed to her feelings.

"It was not a nice thing for you to do, Aïcha. I thought you were a good little girl. Didn't you know how uneasy I would be about you?"

The child looked up.

"There was no need to be uneasy — Aïcha is nothing. I am going to tell thee — Thou wilt not be angry? — At thy house I am very happy but there are so many things to do every moment — the baby's walk, his bath, his soup. Aïcha has to keep watching the clock and this gives her a head-ache. And then, at thy house there are too many stewpans, too many dishes to wash. Thou sayest, 'Aïcha, thou art so well-fed here!' — but thou seest what thy good *tagines* did to Aïcha. When I eat only *kessera* I had no warfare in my stomach. And not only that — between thy stone walls Aïcha stifles. If she stays, she will die. — Let her go. . . ."

There was nothing to do but accede to her request. She went off assuring her mistress that she loved her like a mother and weeping copiously.

But right now, she is happy. On the wild *bled* where she had left her heart, again she guards the sheep.

RAMADAN

CHAPTER XVIII

RAMADAN

I am in luck! — I was able to get back to Marrakech just at the opening night of *Ramadan*.

Well before the narrow thread of a moon floats into the sky, I take up my post of observation on the hotel roof. I must not miss one feature of the spectacle that awaits me. My friends had warned me, " You wait and see — *Ramadan* is dazzling."

It is more than that — it is like a fairy-tale vision. There is not a roof below me without its group of festive women. To bedeck themselves, to set their neighbors marveling and make them envy, they have robbed their chests of all their silks, their caskets of every jewel. They may be lacking in what we call a sense of proportion, but so much the better! This first night of *Ramadan* must be unique among all other nights.

Under a sky of pale limpidity, women and children form glowing groups, bouquets of hardy colors. Rose-corals and purples contrast with sapphire-blue, almond-green with orange-yellow, with nasturtium.

One golden *caftan* glitters like a second sun ; on another, all silvery, marvelous sea-waves seem to break and expand. When the children chase each other from roof to roof they make all the colors of a rainbow that forms and breaks. Elbows on the parapets, faces lifted toward the east, from that distance each woman appears a divine Tanagra figurine. Rockets mount in the air, the cries of *you-you*, the noise of *tam-tams*.

A radiant dying light is melted over everything. A soft breeze gently balances the long plumes of the palms. On the horizon the high summits of the Atlas take on the appearance of pyramids, of a table spread for some fabulous sacrifice ; an incomparable decoration, one of the noblest in the world, for it has both grandeur and simplicity.

· · · · · · ·

Lella Rahama has invited me to take tea with her this afternoon. It required my to-morrow's departure to excuse this breach of the *caïda*. During *Ramadan* no visits are received in the daytime.

Her son, Si Abd el Aziz, has come to find me at my hotel. Lella Rahama's house is situated not far from the blessed *Koutoubia* whose shadow casts fortune on all good believers.

At one time this quarter of the city was bustling with activity. About the old tower of prayer and its mosque, two hundred booksellers alone had their stalls and sold their learned manuscripts.

What desolation has passed over the place since! There is a native account for it that one may believe or not. A certain sultan having dared to massacre at their prayers a group of rebels who had taken refuge in the mosque, the indignant counsel of *Oulemas* ordered, as a means of purifying the place, the demolishing of that part of the temple where the sacrilege took place.

During the succeeding centuries this part of the city has looked like an immense arid field. The curse of God seems indeed to have fallen upon it.

Then came the Europeans. Another curse! Houses of many stories and having " all the modern conveniences " were erected.

Only a single palace is not out of place in the scene. It is that of the general commanding the region. Its ceilings extend to flat roofs, its walls of purple masonry are flowered over with bougainvillaea. To delight those within, sweet-smelling gardens steep in the sun.

Abd el Aziz and I walk along side by side. However strong the heat may burn, my companion is still in his winter *djellaba*, and at every step the heels of his *babouches* click on the hard, dried ground.

An auto passes, another, still another. The dust rises. The color of blood, it mounts in thick clouds and falls back in a rain of hard grains that cut the eyes and irritate the throat. The shining light is darkened. Everything around us disappears — the giant Atlas that upholds the sky on its shoulder, the *Koutoubia* with its emerald and turquoise tiles.

Asphyxiated, blinded, groaning, I exclaim, " Allah never made your country for autos, Abd el Aziz. . . . He made it for camels and asses."

But my young guide, who is ambitious to own his own Ford or Citroen, returns stolidly, " Autos are comfortable."

Aflame with light the square of Djemaa el F'na opens up before us. Under awnings with hanging flaps like those of the card castles that children build, the native merchants seek an illusory shade. The crowd is fairly silent but *tam-tams* resound. The air gives off a strong odour of old leather, garlic, sweat and fruit.

Advance is made by precautionary stages. Standing or seated on the ground itself, spectators form large circles around the snake-charmers, the fire-swallowers, and the *chleuh* dancers with their pretty gestures that are a bit too pretty.

A couple of giant negroes have joined forces to attract the silly ones. Their brown and white striped *djellabas* are opened above their ebony chests.

Planted on his big feet and as if rooted from them, the older interrogates his companion in a thundering voice. He puts to him a series of questions that seem to me the most ridiculously childish riddles, but they are of profound interest to the faithful of simple heart, pressed one against the other to listen. They ascribe to them a deeper meaning, connecting them with questions of religion.

" How does a believer with both arms amputated, go about making his ablutions? " demands the black who takes the rôle of schoolmaster.

A moment of silence as if he were plunged in deep thought, then the " pupil " answers,

" He has someone else make them for him."

To stand still, if it be only for a moment, to hold motionless under the sun's atrocious burning, is to me a diabolic punishment. The shaded street of banks spreads before us. Abd el Aziz and I turn into it.

He tells me about his family.

" My father died when I was a little fellow. I do not even recall him. I had an older brother of twenty ; he was married. His wife died, and he also died last year. He left six orphans, three boys and three girls. My mother is bringing them up. It is hard for an old woman, but Hadra helps her."

[213]

" Who is Hadra? "

" The eldest. She is sixteen."

" Is she pretty? "

" There is nothing lovelier under the sun of the ' Seven Saints.' A flock of sheep would stop eating to look at her."

A question mounts to my lips. Perhaps the *caïda* forbids my asking it. That would never do — if I began to bow to the *caïda*, I, a traveler and an inquisitive one, would risk passing many an interesting thing without even suspecting it was there.

I ask, avoiding a direct glance at Abd el Aziz in order not to add to the embarrassment I might cause him,

" Abd el Aziz, are you married? "

" Not yet."

" I understood that the Prophet ordained a believer to marry and found a family as soon as he could? "

Abd el Aziz smiled. " Is it my fault? "

Intrigued, I went further — and oh certainly this is contrary to the *caïda*.

" You mean you'd like to marry and cannot? "

" How can I? In Morocco, as everywhere else, things have become so much more difficult! "

Two hay-laden camels suddenly fill up the narrow street. We throw ourselves into the nearest alley to let them pass. Abd el Aziz resumes,

" One must have *flouss* to marry."

" You have that, by the grace of God."

" Yes, but not enough. Listen: Thou wouldst not have me marry a girl who was not of my own class, who was, even, not a bit above me. That is something that a Nazarene does not have to think about when he goes to marry, but which counts above everything with a Moslem."

" How do you mean? "

" By Allah, I mean the dowry that must be paid to the girl's parents. Not that we buy our wives as you people so readily believe. A Moslem father no more sells his daughter than a Christian buys a husband for his. The dowry deposited by the young man simply serves to repay his fiancée's family for the expense that she puts them to — the bride's trousseau, the carpets and mattresses for the new household and a thousand purchases besides.''

More camels and donkeys whose leader bawls out his resounding '' *Balek, balek !* ''

Abd el Aziz is undisturbed in his figuring.

'' I've counted the thing up. There's no way out of it but that I must deposit at least thirty thousand francs for a dowry.''

To me it doesn't seem like too much to pay to get a girl of good family, but Allah puts a seal on my lips.

'' And that's not all,'' proceeds Abd el Aziz. '' There's the question of the necessary gifts. . . At least four or five thousand francs.''

I add up mechanically. '' That comes to thirty-five thousand.''

'' Don't think it! It comes to at least forty, for there's the matter of cost for the wedding feast. Forty thousand francs! Where do you expect me to find it? ''

I gesture helplessly. '' I certainly don't know.''

Abd el Aziz adds, '' Of course I have property. It is well situated and valuable. I could sell a piece of it. But my property brings in my income, and my wife then would simply be a cause of dispensing it. You surely see why I am not able to marry.''

From the point of view of arithmetic it is impossible to contradict him ; Abd el Aziz is correct ; but every question has several aspects. I begin,

'' If you were married, your wife would love you, she would make you happy.''

My young companion throws me an ironical glance. It is quite plain that he judges me naïve for my age.

'' Do you know how many divorces, how many repudiations, there are each year in Marrakech? ''

'' Many, I'm sure of that. You repudiate your unhappy wives as easily, as carelessly, as you leave your *babouches* at the door when you enter a room.''

'' Our unhappy wives! You mean their unhappy husbands! By Allah, you don't know the reasons brought to bear on us.''

'' Tell them.''

'' It would take me from now to the hour of *Moghreb*.''

[215]

" Tell some of them, then."

" I will give you a few examples.   My friends are almost all married. When they announced their marriage everybody drank to their happiness, for it really seemed they were doing a fine thing.   They had aspired to, or rather their mother had aspired for them, to a rich girl of good family connections.   But scarcely was the marriage concluded than the girl drew from her social superiority the right to manage everything her own way. No more liberty for the man.   If he went out for a moment, if he returned a little late, there were suspicious questions, scenes, clamor — ' Where hast thou been? — Where didst thou come from? — Who was with thee?' "

" Your friends should have married women of their own class."

" That flatters the vanity less.   But vanity aside, I'll admit certain unions are profitable."

There we were exactly at the same point as before.   I attempted to reason in a different light.

" A wife should give you children."

But my argument is valueless.   It is a *Roumiya's* argument.   Retorting to it, in two phrases Abd el Aziz has measured the abyss that separates the two civilizations.

" Children?   Why should I need to be married to have children?   No matter what slave bears them for me, they will be legitimate.   With us it is only paternity that counts."

With this Abd el Aziz stops at the porch of a house in one of the city's oldest streets.   Its cedar doorway is flanked on the right by a stone bench. Here the " master of things " sometimes comes out to take the air, here the porter bears the visitors company who wait their turn to enter, while a slave warns the women to retire to their apartments.

We go first through the passage, then into the patio.   It is a large one but with a saddening air, without bright tiles or a fountain.

In one of the inner rooms waits Lella Rahama with her two granddaughters.   She makes a high ceremony of receiving me, dressed in a *caftan* of sober brown.   A negress near her, as broad as she is long, gives me her hand with the same familiarity as one of the family.   In fact she is one of them — she is Abd el Aziz's *dada*.

Lella Rahama has me take a seat in *el bahou*.   The court opens before us like a green yard.   On either side the doorway the two girls sit face to face.

They have left off all their jewelry to mark that the month we have entered on is a time of penitence.   In order to prevent the holes for their heavy ear-rings from closing up in the meantime, they have ingenuously pulled twists of cotton through the openings, whose vivid rose spreads out at the ear lobes into comical-looking loops.

Abd el Aziz was not exaggerating.   The eldest of his nieces is so beautiful that at first it is almost disconcerting.   Her profile is of flawless purity. Lifting the black fringe of her lids, her glance dazzles you and charms you with its tenderness.   When she dips her shy head to her shoulder it is the movement of a turtle dove.

In comparison her sister is all that she is not.   Perfect beauty creates a sort of waste around it, and that is perhaps why beautiful women are not more loved by other women.

The third day of Ramadan ends that afternoon.   Since four o'clock that morning none of my hosts have eaten or drunk.

Slipping down on one of the mattresses, young Abd el Aziz yawns and draws out his watch every other minute to see how much longer he must wait for the sound of the liberating cannon.

" Allah, Allah ! " he sighs, " these first days are the worst punishment. One's stomach is not accustomed to it.   And then there's the lack of sleep. Allah, Allah ! I've got such a headache this moment that I'm almost crazy.   Everything in me is empty, everything."

The women, and it is not so astonishing, show more courage.   In the patio there is a little girl, a darling of a child, who never stops running back and forth.   Each time she passes the door she turns her head our way.

It is not to see if we are admiring her dress, made of a scrap of cotton in a fresh canary-yellow, but because she has fasted to-day for the first time in her life.

" We permitted it in order to get her accustomed to it," explains Lella Rahama.   " She is so proud of being treated like a grown-up person that she wants everybody in the world to know it."

Meanwhile, in a corner of the court, an old woman, a slave, sits folded on her feet.   Her great age exempts her from fasting, but soon, she knows, she will be asked to render an account of her life. She wishes to present herself purified, having obtained God's pardon for all her faults.

"I would be ashamed in God's presence," she tells me, croaking, "if I had not observed *Ramadan*. May I be able to keep it up to the time I die!"

Once more Abd el Aziz consults his watch.

"How many minutes now, Abd el Aziz?"

"Sixty-five."

"If you would occupy yourself with something the time would seem less long."

"Allah! I haven't got strength enough!"

"The women are showing you an example."

"They are accustomed to suffering. However, I realize they are more tired than I am. They are the ones *Ramadan* is hardest on. I went to bed, myself, after the third prayer and slept almost three hours."

"While your mother and your nieces and the slaves —"

"They went to bed yesterday evening at about six o'clock as usual, but they had to get up at midnight."

He concluded with a yawn, "It is obligatory."

There could be nothing more contagious than to see him yawn. Yawning myself, I ask,

"Why is it obligatory?"

"They have the meals to prepare. Each city has its customs for waking them up. At Rabat a beggar runs through the streets beating a drum, at some of the other places he blows a trumpet. At Fez — But is all this interesting to you?" he asks all at once and, as usual, yawning.

"Very much."

"Allah, Allah! I see what you are. You are one of these ladies who wants to know everything. All right, my mother will explain it all to you. She is a *Fascia* and besides — I'm not able to."

Full length on the cushions, as though he had been laid out, Abd el Aziz yawns and yawns again.

Then she whose name means " the miserable," Lella Rahama, takes it upon herself to continue the conversation.

"At Fez the believer charged with waking the women is called the *dakak*."

" Do you know what that means? " yawns Abd el Aziz.

" No."

" One who knocks."

" The position of *dakak* is hereditary," goes on Lella Rahama. " He receives a small sum as remuneration from the *Habous* and each inhabitant contributes toward paying the *dakak* of his quarter by handing over fifty centimes with seventeen measures of wheat."

" The *dakak* goes from house to house. He has a hammer with which he strikes each door, calling,

" ' Oh ye faithful, awake, awake! . . . It is high time to prepare your repasts to keep Ramadan in the peace of God. . . . ' "

I ask, " At what hour must the women be waked? "

" At least by five o'clock," comes from the depths of Abd el Aziz's cushions. " *Ramadan* is a time of privation during the day, but of rejoicing during the night. From sunset to sunrise there are continual receptions. Think of all the *tagines* that must be prepared and all the cakes to bake! For eight hours the women are up, the ' mistress of things ' as well as the slaves, for the ' mistress of things ' must give the orders. If she can sleep for an hour or two toward the end of the morning, it is all that she has a right to expect."

However absorbing the question of *Ramadan* may be, there is something else that piques Lella Rahama's curiosity. Not once have I entered a harem without someone asking at the very first,

" Art thou married? Hast thou children? "

Even the nuns do not escape this interrogation, " Why hast thou never married? — Thou art young."

By a natural ascent this type of conversation leads Lella Rahama to speak of the husband she has lost.

I wonder sometimes if there is a single exception among Moroccan widows? They tell me there is not and I believe it. However, I must say that after twenty years of widowhood this one speaks of her lost lord with the same genuine emotion as if she had just laid him away.

Getting up, she unhooks from the wall a gilt-framed portrait. It is an enlarged photograph of him who was Si Taher.

" Look at him," she mourns. " One would have said that he knew

[221]

he was going to die and that he felt that he must leave a souvenir of himself to me and the children. He had never wanted to have his likeness taken ; he decided to do it just a few weeks before he died.

"See how handsome he was and how young! Never had he been sick before. But each man bears his destiny written on his brow. In his hour Allah will summon him home.

"So many people are astonished that I never remarried. When one has such a husband as he, how can one accept another? Where find his equal? Allah never made two like him. He not only had beauty and strength but he had a great heart. He was the best and most generous of men. Since I lost him I have never known a happy day. . . ."

Lella Rahama sighed with eyes tear-filled, adding,

"To honor me, to show what confidence he had in me, in his will he named me my children's guardian. Thou sayest, 'Is that not customary?' — Among Nazarenes it is, but not among Moslems. Even if I had wanted to marry again that proof of my husband's esteem and affection would have kept me from it."

A moment more she stares sadly at the portrait, then as an appeal to one no longer here, her lips murmur,

"My dear, dear lord. . . ."

Motioning to Hadra and her sister who are watching her, I try to say, "These little granddaughters will be your consolation. These children whom Allah has 'dropped in thy lap,' you must cherish them. You must find Hadra a good husband."

The older woman shook her head.

"Oh my grief! What art thou saying? — Hadra must stay at home! She must help me bring up her brothers and sisters. Her sister will marry, *Inch Allah*, but Hadra is necessary here. She is a good, devoted girl."

Abd el Aziz, whom we thought asleep, wakes to yawn and add,

"Hadra was betrothed when her father died. Her fiancé was a friend of mine. I decided that we would give him Zohra, the younger. Because she is so young Zohra can't give the same service in the house as her sister. And besides, she hasn't her qualities."

Abd el Aziz was expressing himself in French. Lella Rahama did not understand what he was saying, but she guessed that we were speaking of his nieces ; she confirmed the decision taken.

" Zohra will be married after *Ramadan*, if it be God's will.   But no husband for Hadra.   Allah has written it over her.   Allah is the all-wise ! "

Hadra makes no response to her grandmother's words ; her lids droop, she does not cease her gentle smiling.

But what a laceration must have appeared in her soul when she was told that she must let her sister supplant her, because her rôle of elder sister demanded it and — what irony — because she was the better of the two.

She had made no protest.   She sat with her constant smile, with her sweet virginal air, on the soft woolen carpet beside us — but in the middle of the night, when only the far-off cock was crowing, who could know the silent tears that she let fall. . . .

Celibacy imposed by circumstances and by one's own people represents for those of her race the saddest possible fate.   Her youth will be passed in devotion to her brothers ; when they are grown her beauty will be faded; she will grow old in the household like one already half dead.

One of the slaves had brought in tea.   My hosts with big eyes watch me drink a sip of it and crumble my cake.   One makes haste eating alone and besides I hurried to shorten the punishment that those who surrounded me were undergoing.

Little by little the day had darkened.   One time more Abd el Aziz consults his watch, one time more he yawns.   But an unexpected spectacle distracts me.

Across the patio, and coming toward us in the crystal air, was a group of four sumptuous dolls, the most enchanting, the most dazzling that it is possible to imagine.   They advanced in a line and sometimes they bumped against each other.   Their strange attire was as much in their way as their gigantic and unwieldy head dresses.   They glided forward with tiny steps on their shining *babouches*, hesitating, balancing on their slim hips.

Carried away, I demanded of Abd el Aziz, " Who are these charming creatures? "

" My mother's daughter's daughters. It is the custom among wealthy Moroccan families that for three days the little girls who have not yet observed *Ramadan*, are prepared by the *g'nafa* as if for their marriage. They are fixed up with henna and *kohl* and everything."

Arrived at the open door the marvelous dolls stop short, abashed. No one had told them that a Nazarene was making a visit. The smallest, who could not be more than three, sets up a piercing cry.

All *Roumiyas* are ogresses. She knows it. If they have white skin it is because they eat the flesh of little children — the *dada* said so.

Without waiting to hear anything different, the little thing flees to hide behind the *g'nafa* whose rotundity affords a screen.

With more courage than she could muster, her sisters and cousin gravely advance to kiss their grandmother's hand and their uncle's.

Untiringly I study and admire the charming and magnificent details of their costumes. One wears a *caftan* of green velvet braided over every inch of its surface. Her little head is crowned with tall black ostrich plumes that undulate graciously with her movements.

Another is dressed in a robe of turquoise blue clouded in silver-pailleted tulle ; a kerchief of rose and lilac knotted on her black hair sways a long fringe on her thin little shoulders.

But the most beautiful of the three is the eldest one. Before long she will be observing *Ramadan* and already she bears herself with the airs of a great lady. Made of a golden tissue with purplish high lights, her costume puffs out above the hips as if distended by a crinoline ; her sleeves, so long that they trail on the ground, are tucked up at the sides like wings. A gold bandeau set with emeralds is twisted around her forehead ; covering her ears, falling clear to her shoulders, she wears a hair-net of real pearls and precious stones.

The three little creatures seat themselves side by side on the floor. Their wide petticoats stand out around them like a bell. Thanks to their appearance the whole thing has taken on a tinge of enchantment — the realization of a Persian folk-tale, an unbelievable fairy story.

They hold themselves just so without budging. Their faces are deliciously painted ; eyebrows so elongated by *kohl* that they seem to run into their ears. They are hieratic and vividly alive and I have never seen

anything more charming than the expression of fitting gravity imprinted on their round little faces under the arched brows.

The hour of *Moghreb* approaches, the hour for ascending to the roofs.

Once more the little dolls cross the patio under the *g'nafa's* care, their little hands holding up their heavy petticoats. Ruby colored, sapphire, emerald, they look like precious birds escaped from some marvelous aviary. Their little shoulders glisten, their little breasts shimmer and one is astonished not to hear them chirp.

They get all tangled up in the narrow staircase whose high steps are difficult for short legs to mount. The porter has already opened the door to the roof with his big iron key.

Armchairs have been arranged beforehand and cushions put in them, many cushions to increase the height of the seats.

With infinite precaution each child is hoisted into the throne erected for her and her petticoats carefully adjusted.

The sun is setting in a nimbus of rays. The emerald's facets catch the light, the orient magnifies the pearls. A little passing breeze shakes the tremulous beauty of the ostrich plumes set in a diadem on a tiny head.

Beyond the *Koutoubia* a minaret seems to float painted in mauve. Toward the east, in the milky paleness, are other minarets that seem as unreal and as suavely drawn.

Until the end of the day, until the first chill falls from the night sky, these ravishing dolls stay on exhibition. They make no gesture, speak no word — the *caïda* forbids it — but their eyes shine with a still delight. Lella Rahama who has joined us whispers,

" These little children, we beautify them to make them happy. It is necessary that the rays of their happiness be high enough to mount up to God and rejoice His heart."

One last time before I go I study the radiant spectacle whose like my eyes had never seen before.

How pretty these babies in their naïve joy, and how tender and full of grace is this fierce and disenchanted religion of Islam when it concerns itself with little children. . . .

NOTES

NOTES

Page   6. "day of days."   An outstanding day.
Page   6. "gazelle-horns."   Pastry of finely ground almonds.
Page   6. "wear the turban."   When a boy becomes of age.
Page   7. "at the last figs."   At the last harvest of the figs.
Page 18. "eat of the stick."   A beating.
Page 18. "went to the pardon of Allah."   (Allah — The Adorable, Supreme Being.) Died in the Mohammedan faith.
Page 19. "she was born with a palm-tree on her head."   Born lucky.
Page 19. "veil of pride."   Veil worn at a marriage.   Bride's veil.
Page 24. "as a wind in a cage."   Easily extinguished.
Page 24. "may the sea be over thee."   So much the worse for thee.
Page 25. "belongs to the couch."   The child belongs to the father.
Page 25. "had blown it through his nose."   Marked resemblance — spit image.
Page 39. "hand of Fatma."   An amulet worn for protection against the evil eye.
Page 42. "Allah will open to them."   God will open to thee another door; a phrase to get rid of a beggar.
Page 49. "daughter of joy."   A prostitute.
Page 52. "Allah has written it over her."   It has been decreed by Allah; there is no revoking the sentence.
Page 60. "tear up the card."   Break the marriage contract.
Page 64. "gazelle-blood color."   Bright red.
Page 64. "mistress of things."   The head woman of the household.
Page 68. "the Sultan's corners."   The place of honor.
Page 74. "The mercy of Allah."   A formula of repentence.
Page 99. "making the *burnous* sweat."   Obtaining a day's work for a day's pay.
Page 139. "seven fig days."   A honeymoon.
Page 157. "Seven Saints."   Seven sages, or seven wise men.   Saints of the seven saints were the protectors of the city of Marrakech where a mosque is erected to them.   There they are known as "the marabouts" in houses.
Page 159. "Fajr to Acha."   Moslems have five daily prayers.   First is that of dawn: FAJR; the second, one hour after noon: DHUHR; the third, 'ASR,

taking place of midway between the zenith and sunset; the fourth at sunset, MAGHRIB; fifth and last 'ACHA, when night has fallen, marking the evening meal.

Page 159. "observed Ramadan." The ninth month of the Mahometan year is the Mussulman's Lent or holy month. It is kept by fasting in the daytime and feasting at night. Only those of adolescent years keep this fast; girls at the age of fourteen.

Page 164. "curse Satan." Formula addressed to those who dispute. The popular belief that Satan inhabits the souls of the angry.

Page 173. "anger of the Seven Saints." To commit a crime in the neighborhood of the mosque of the Seven Saints in Marrakech is to arouse the anger of the Seven Saints.

Page 183. "master of things." The head of the house.

Page 183. "the house." Expression for "thy wife" as she must not be mentioned.

Page 187. "City of Seven Saints." Marrakech, where the Seven Saints are housed.

Page 188. "sacred month." Ramadan.

Page 189. "sent off like a sack of sweet potatoes." Sent off alone.

Page 189. "shame of the face." Embarrassment.

Page 191. "sons of Cham." Negroes.

Page 192. "Farce de Maître Parhelin." Name of a French farce.

Page 192. "L'Agnelet." Little lamb. Name of a French play.

Page 195. "daughter of my master." Exclamation common to women.

Page 200. "In the bosom of Allah." In paradise.

Page 210. "Counsel of the Oulemas." Learned men.

GLOSSARY

GLOSSARY

acha — evening prayer. The fifth prayer of the day.

Abd-Salam — prayer of peace.

Abl ul Aziz — name meaning servant of the Mighty (God).

adouls — lawyers, notary public.

Agadir — name of a town.

Ahmed — name of a man; the praised one.

Aisha — the favorite wife of Mohammed, the living.

Ait-el-Kebir — the great festival, follows seven weeks after the end of Ramadan.

Al-adra — the Virgin Mary.

al Baramki — was one of the viziers (ministers) of Haroun al Rashid, celebrated for his riches and generosity.

Ali — proper name (noun).

Allah — God. There are 99 names for Allah in the Mohammedan religion which are repeated by believers when saying the 99 beads of the rosary.

Andalous — (Mosque of) Spanish Arabic (Andalusian-Arabic) mosque.

arifa — (guard) female watcher.

arousa — bride.

Ashkoun — who is there? — who is it?

ayal (iyal) — harem, family, folk, household. The word "harem" is a Turkish expression. Moroccans use the word "iyal" which designates the women's apartments.

Azrou — name of a town.

Bab-Doukkala — the Gate of Doukkala.

Bab Fetouh — name of a gate; the gate of victory.

babouches (babouj) — native shoes or slippers.

balek balek (balak!) — look out! (Fais attention!)

baraka — blessing; said at the end of a meal.

barak Allah fik — may God bless you!

baroud — gun-powder; (by extension: trouble).

Batoul — the lazy one.

Beja — name of a place.

benikas (benika) — little tabouret used as desk.

ben — son of.

bent — daughter of.

bezzaf — lots, very much.

bled (bilad) — country.

Boua sidi — my lord or master.

burnous — hooded cloak.

caftan — long garment fastened by a girdle(mostly worn by Jews).

caid (kaid) — military leader ; governor of a district.

cadi (kadi) — judge.

Caïd Omar — chief Omar.

caïda (kaida) — a leader (feminine).

casa — house (Spanish).

chacals — jackals ; ropes.

chaouch (shaouch) — corporal.

Chaouia — name of a Berber province.

chéchia (fez) — head-dress.

cherif (sherif) — noble ; descendant of Muhammad.

cherifa (sherifa) — noble woman ; descendant of Muhammad.

cherif Moulay Ibrahim — my lord Ibrahim.

cherifian — Moroccan (belonging to Moroccan government).

chitane (sheitan) — Satan ; devil.

Chleuh — a Berber tribe.

chorfas — shurafa — plural for cherif.

chouari (shouari) — double basket, or handbag.

chraa (sheri'a) — religious law which the kadis apply.

couffins — hand bags.

couscous (kouskous) — typical North African dish.

dada — nurse.

dakak (dakkaki in Tunis, tabbal) — a man who wakes up the Muslims during Ramadan about half an hour before daybreak, so they could eat their meal to last till sunset (literally : a "knocker" or drum-beater).

Djamaa el F'na — provincial square of Marrakech.

djellaba — tunic (woman's).

djerid (jerid) — palm leaf ; also palm tree.

djinn — genie or evil spirit.

douar — village of desert people.

doue (dawa') — medicine or remedy.

doun (doum) — low palm.

douros — Spanish *duro* — 5 peseta coin.

el bahou (al bahou) — alcove ; or anything spacious, or a hiding place.

el Dehli — the golden.

el Hadj — the pilgrim.

fabor — Spanish "favor" ; tip.

faqih — one who knows the Islamic law.

Fasi — natives of Fez.

Fasiya — a woman native of Fez.

Fatima — very usual name. As firstborn sons are called Muhammad, the eldest girl is called Fatima. By extension, all women, especially a slave.

fejer (fajr) — dawn, daybreak.

ferragiats (farragiyat) — over-tunics of women.

fez — head-dress.

flouss (fulous) — cash, money.

fondouks — inns, hotels.

gandourah(s) — man's lower garment.

gehenna — hell.

g'nafa — match-maker.

gnaoua — negro.

gnaouas — negroes.

habous — religious property (so-called Wakfs) mortmain.

Hadj Kaddour — very powerful.

Hadra — the proper name of a maid.

haïk — cloak.

haitis — hangings.

Hajeb — name of a village.

Halima — proper name meaning "sweet," "dreamy," "the gentle."

hammam — the baths.

harira — thick pottage; soup which Moroccans eat in the morning.

harkas — light cavalry.

Hassan — proper name meaning "pretty."

henna — coloring powder, vegetable matter.

Ia — Oh!

Idriss — name of a man, a saint, probably the prophet Elijah.

inch'allah! (insh'Allah) — God willing.

Iyal — the word harem is a Turkish expression. Moroccans use the word "iyal" (families, folks) which designates the women's apartments.

jalika — the grieved one, she who suffers pain.

Jami — mosque.

Jami ul F'na — principal square of Marrakech.

jellaba — noisy woman.

jellabia — tunic.

Kaddour — proper name.

kanoun — open stove.

kaouada (kawwada) — go-between (feminine) Spanish; alcahueta; procuress.

Karouyne — university and mosque in Fez.

Kawwada — go-between.

kessara — unleavened cakes.

Kessaria — name of a place, probably Caeserea.

Khadidja — name of the first nine wives of Mohammad.

Khadouj — proper name.

khalifa — caliph, or lieutenant, or substitute.

Kheita — proper name.

Kheïra — blessing of God, the good one, name of a woman.

kif, kif (keef keef) (just like) — the same thing.

kobs — mugs, bucket.

kohl — kohl; cosmetic used to blacken the eyebrows.

Koran — holy book of the Mohammedans.

koubbas (kubba) — room; dome of a room; and by extension all rooms.

Koutoubia — Mosque in Marrakech, tomb of a Prophet.

leila — night.

lella — name of a woman — title like "Mrs." in English.

lellas — ladies.

litham — a muffler for the mouth.

Mabrouka — the welcome one — the blessed one.

macache (ma kansh) — there is none at all (*il n'y a pas*).

Maghreb — Morocco — *i.e.* the Western lands of the Moslems.

Mahjoub — name; the hidden one.

makhraz — needle; awl.

makhzen (makhzan) — store room, magazine, in Morocco: palace of the Sultan.

Malika — queen.

Marrakechi — native of Marrakech.

Marrakish — Morocco, also city of the same name.

ma shay — nothing doing; nothing.

mehallas (mahalla) — a city quarter, a camp.

mellah (millah) — religious community (race only by extension, as for example, Jews, who happen to have a different millah).

Merzoug — the patron saint of the negroes.

meskina (maskina) — poor woman (used with the connotation of pity).

meskines — the poor.

Messaouda — the lucky one.

Mohammad ben Moktar — the chosen one.

Mokhraznis — name of a body of troops (like chasseurs, tirailleurs).

Moktar — Si Ali Moktar, the chosen one.

moualinadour — guardian, watchman.

moulad (mouloud) — festival; birthday of Muhammad especially.

Moulay — my Lord.

Moulay Idris — my lord Idris, a saint of Maghreb; also name of a holy city.

moutchachou (Spanish muchacho) — boy.

muezzin (muedhin) — announcer of prayer.

Muhammad — Mohammed.

Nazarenes — Christians.

Omar — father-in-law of Mohammed.

ouarrah (ouakhkha) — certainly, perfectly, decidedly.

oued — water course, valley, river.

Oulad Saïd — name of a tribe. Sons or children of Said.

pasha — a title.

pesetas — Spanish coin.

qarqbas (qarqabas) — castanets.

Rabat — town and fortress.

Rahama — the merciful.

raita — garment or cloth.

raitas — castanets.

Ramadan — holy month of fast.

rei — money (Portuguese rei).

rezza — turban.

riads — gardens, riadh — walled garden or meadow.

Roumiya — foreign woman, or Christian woman.

Roumiyas — ogresses.

saadian — belonging to the Moroccan dynasty, 16th to 17th century.

sadecq (sadaq) — dowry, which the man's parents give to the girl's parents.

salaam — peace, salutation of peace.

sallam — to salute.

sebennias (sebenia) — head shawl for women.

semola — millet — a dish.

serouals (sirwal) — trousers, pantaloons.

Sheitan — Satan.

Sheria — religious law which the Kadis apply.

Si — our title of Mr.

Si Abd el Azez — the servant of the powerful.

Si Abderrahamen — servant of the merciful.

Si Ahmed ben Omar — praised one.

Si Ibrahim — ben Lhassen, son of Hassen.

sidi, baba — my lord, father.

sidi, sayyidi — my lord, my master.

souak — pomegranate peel.

Souira — native son of Maghador.

[238]

souks (souk) — bazar, market.

Soudan — a country.

sous — licorice, a district in Morocco (Sous).

Stouka — name of a place.

sumoula — old garment.

surahs — chapter of the Koran.

tabeeba — doctress (Spanish: curandera).

tagine, tagines — tagin — simmered stews.

Tahir — name of a woman; pure.

tajer (tajir) — merchant, often implies wealth.

tam tam — a drum.

Taroudant — Berber tribe.

thair — slayers of persons (relation) in vengeance.

thalaba — garment.

thoba — shirt.

Timbuctoo — city in the Soudan.

toubeba — (herb medicine woman).

ya, sidi — Oh my lord!

Yakout — Ruby, the name of a woman.

Yousseff (Yusuf) — Joseph.

Zamita — a grave, sedate, or calm woman, proper name.

zelligis — tiles (Spanish: azulejo).

Zemeb — name of a saint.

Zohra — Venus (star), proper name of a woman.